t!ts out slits out

emma elizabeth

Get 'em out, gals <3

content notes

This is a spicy alien romance that includes:
Public nudity (nudist resort)
Mentions of sex work (positive/respectful)
Adopted family (love interest)
Use of "plan B" birth control
Discussions of pregnancy

Featured tropes include:

Fisting
Tentacles
Fated mates
Fake dating
"Virgin" FMC
Sexting
"Try harder"
Squirting

chapter one

Stella could not believe she had agreed to this. Her three friends sat across from her on the shuttle, laughing because Lenny had said "Pee you there" instead of "see you there" when she got off the phone just now. Stella felt laughter bubbling in her chest as well, but her apprehension was overpowering it.

So, she stared out the window and watched as the neon space station grew larger and larger.

Dana, Lenny, and Marie were on the shuttle with Stella, and their other friend, Taylor, was already at the resort.

She knew her friends had meant well in planning this birthday trip for her—they wanted her to experience all life had to offer. That included hooking up with hot people, apparently.

"I'm so excited to see Taylor, it's been way too long." Marie took a sip of her complimentary mojito.

"Seriously, they're always so busy. I can't believe it's

taking an off-world vacation for them to make time final-ly." Dana laughed as she spoke.

Dana had been Stella's best friend since childhood. They'd been together through thick and thin, even through the coming-out glow-ups of their mid-twenties. She and Dana had been awkward little girls, but now they were both settled in themselves more fully. Dana's gangly legs had grown into elegant, long limbs, which now were folded into her chair unceremoniously. Dana's dark brown eyes were fixed on Stella–she'd been caught staring. Stella stuck her tongue out at Dana, and Dana returned the gesture without hesitation.

Lenny sat to Dana's left and looked over at her girl-friend sitting there with her tongue out. She rolled her eyes and laughed. Lenny and Dana had gotten together about two years ago, and Stella loved Lenny like a sister now, too. Lenny was so effortlessly cool–even now, sitting on the shuttle with her pink-tipped black hair in a messy bun, she looked chic.

"I hope this is a great experience for you, Stella. You deserve it, you know." Marie said, smiling at Stella. Marie had joined their little group when Stella had met her at work a few years back. They'd become fast friends, bonding over all of their crazy coworkers. When Lenny had suggested this trip to help Stella "have some goddamn birthday sex for once", Marie had been thrilled–she had always wanted to come to this specific resort, apparently.

Stella had been "too busy" for a relationship for years.

In high school and college, she had used her studies as her excuse–she needed scholarships and the best way to get those was to study hard and stay focused, so no dating for her. As an adult with a job, avoiding it was ... harder to explain. Her friends had tried to set her up with people, but nothing had ever really taken off. So here Stella was, turning 28, and she'd never even fucked anyone.

Now the prospect of doing it made her so anxious that it was hard to think about. Who would possibly be nice and normal about a 28-year-old virgin? She wasn't a prude–she read books and knew what to do in theory, she just ... hadn't actually done any of it.

She'd kissed boys, but it hadn't really done much for her. Kissing girls had been much, much better. She wondered if kissing an alien would be very different.

"So! When we land, they should take our luggage and show us our rooms. We can take a bit to freshen up, but there's a dinner show tonight, I think we should go to." Lenny said, Dana and Marie nodding.

"Sounds good."

"What kind of show is it?" Dana asked.

"It's stand-up comedy."

Stella snorted out a laugh. "So the comedian will be naked too? Just up there telling jokes, totally naked."

"Everyone is naked, Stella, that's the whole point." Lenny's lovely, elongated eyes flashed with mirth as she smiled at Stella. Her teasing was always done in good fun.

"Right. See, I understand that, and I'm just struggling to process it, I think." When Stella looked at Dana, she found a mix of sympathy and smugness on Dana's face.

The shuttle gave a slight lurch as they came to a stop. No turning back now. She had just arrived at an alien nudist resort in space.

The girls gathered their things and headed to the front of the shuttle to disembark. When the cabin door slid open, a massive Sozarin stood before them, smiling widely.

Stella wasn't precious about seeing aliens–interplanetary travel had been around for decades, so species other than humans were fairly commonplace even back on Earth. What threw her off was being nearly eye-level with the alien's naked crotch. Their skin was electric purple, glittering slightly in the light of the space station behind them. They were mostly humanoid, but their muscles were incredibly defined, and they had delicate ridges that adorned their cheekbones, forearms, and thighs. Oh, and a tail–they had a tail. And there was a massive slit between their legs, and Stella realized in horror she was staring right at it.

"Welcome to Galaxy View Resort! I hope you all are ready to undress and unwind!"

Stella's friends all laughed and cheered in response. Stella sighed and gave a weak "woo!"

Dana took Lenny's hand as she moved to follow their Sozarin host, and Marie fell into step next to Stella.

They made their way down a long hall with the most

aggressively neon pattern Stella had ever seen. She was so hypnotized by it that she didn't even notice when it ended. Marie gripped her wrist with a squeal, and Stella looked up to see a massive rotunda before her. There were areas of white-sand beach where people lounged, surrounded by lush tropical greenery. A massive, perfectly blue pool took up the middle of the space, and humans and aliens dotted it, floating in the crystal waters. The edge of the space had little shops and restaurants–from here she could see a chic coffee spot, an ice cream parlor, and a sports bar.

"I want one of THOSE!" Marie whisper-yelled, pointing at some kind of massive frozen cocktail a human man was holding with both hands, sipping from the bendy straw as he walked back to his friends on the beach.

It was really nice here, Stella could admit that. Everyone was just very, *very* naked.

"This is the main resort pool, as I'm sure you've figured out," their host said with a smile. "Here you'll find a wide range of dining options. If you're interested in any of our more niche experiences, you can find all of the information in our app."

Stella knew that booking time with the escorts was one of the "niche experiences" they were referring to. Nerves tingled through her, and she took a deep breath.

Their host led them through several other long hallways, all with high ceilings and dotted with entrances to various resort amenities–a salon, a bakery, a soda shop, and a sex toy store were a few that Stella happened to notice.

They turned onto a quieter hall lined with numbered doors–finally, the rooms. The thought of having to walk past other people in the hallway of a hotel was awkward enough, but Stella realized that she would have to do it naked here. She fought back a laugh.

"Here we are!" their host said, smiling. Slightly elongated canine teeth gave them the appearance of fangs, which was only slightly unsettling in a customer-service smile.

"Thank you!" Lenny beamed back at their host. They handed Lenny the room keys and nodded before leaving the girls to distribute the keys however they chose.

"Ok, so Dana and I are in 31800, Marie and Taylor in 31801, and Stella in 31802," Lenny said, handing a few key cards to each person as she spoke. "Your app should also open the door for you, but just in case, the keycards are nice to have."

The girls had absolutely insisted that Stella should have her own room for this excursion. They had told her that if she didn't manage to figure out the birthday sex thing on her own, they would hire her one of the escorts the resort was known for. Stella acted like she was less than enthusiastic about this trip, and to a certain extent, she was, but she did want to have that experience of sleeping with someone. She'd never done it, and she was just mostly curious what all the fuss was about. She wasn't sure why they'd had to come all this way, but her friends wanted to do something special for her, and it was sweet. It was just ... a lot.

"Everyone, be ready for dinner in an hour!" Lenny said, and they all nodded before turning to their respective rooms to settle in.

Stella opened the door to find that her bags had already been dropped off, for which she was eternally grateful.

The room was very nice, she had to admit. The layout was similar to what she would have expected from a hotel on Earth, but everything was much more colorful. Shades of glossy neon were on every surface: a bright pink bedspread, green and blue tiles on the floor, purple walls. There was just the one massive bed, a large screen embedded in the wall, a few lamps--but the large sliding glass doors at the end of the room caught her attention. She rose from the bed and stepped over to them, peering out. There was a balcony with a lounge chair and a small end table, but the view nearly took her breath away. The balcony was contained in what appeared to be a glass bubble attached to the side of the station, surrounded by the endlessness of space. The stars were so bright here. She slid the door open hesitantly and stepped onto the balcony. She was out there among the stars--maybe this wouldn't be such a bad way to spend her birthday after all.

Before Stella realized, an hour had passed, and her friends were knocking on her door to leave for dinner and to see that stand-up comedy show. Stella wasn't dressed; she'd lost track of time staring out at space.

"Are you so for real, Stella?" Lenny asked with a laugh.

"I know, I know, I'm sorry," she said, and she really did feel bad. She was a little overwhelmed with the concept of this trip, but she loved that her friends had wanted to do this for her. She just felt like she needed a bit of time before she threw herself into the deep end of this experience.

"Would you guys mind terribly if I did my own thing just tonight? I feel like I need to adjust to being here, and I'm a little tired. Doing a whole sit-down dinner sounds like a lot for me right now."

Marie looked concerned, but nodded without hesitation.

"You promise you're alright?" Dana asked. She knew Stella well enough that this request probably wasn't unexpected.

"Promise. Text me when you guys are done? I might try to find a hot tub to lie in and unwind a bit." Stella smiled at them.

"Oh hell yes, we will join you when the show is over," Lenny said.

Stella gave her friends a wave as they turned to make their way down the hall.

She decided to unpack her bag a bit since they would be there for a whole week. She had still packed clothes because it seemed way too weird not to. She stashed them in a drawer of the dresser that sat under the massive screen on one wall.

Once she had put away her toiletries in the bathroom, she sat on the edge of the bed and pulled her phone out. Lenny had sent them all a link to the resort map in the app, so Stella opened it and searched for a spa or something similar. It looked like there was a small lounge area close by that had exactly what she was looking for—a sauna, a bar, a hot tub, and a cold plunge. It wasn't the main pool area, either, so maybe it would be a bit more of a manageable start to the whole being naked in public thing.

It was one of the strangest experiences of Stella's life to stand up and undress in preparation for leaving her hotel room. Everything about it felt wrong. She laughed at the ridiculousness of this situation. If you had asked her a year ago whether there was a chance she'd end up at a nudist alien resort for her birthday, she would have laughed.

How, exactly, she was going to meet someone to fuck here was beyond her. She wasn't opposed to her friends hiring an escort; it just made her nervous. It honestly might be for the best. They were professionals, and their work was respected; she knew she would be in good hands with one of them. There was something about it that made her feel just a tiny bit disappointed, though. She wanted her first time to be with someone who really wanted her, too. It didn't have to be some kind of love match, but ... just some sort of spark to explore, even if it was just for one night.

Stella was extremely aware of the slight chill of the air on her bare skin as she stepped into the hall. She had her Van Gogh tote bag with her and was wearing her baby-pink flip-flops, but nothing else. Everything felt so ... *jiggly* as she walked. Thankfully, she managed to avoid seeing anyone else alone in the hallway, but when she turned out into the main path that would take her to her little spa area, there were naked people and aliens everywhere she looked.

She took a deep breath and hoped that she would soon become desensitized to it. Everyone else was doing it too; it was good for her. She repeated this to herself over and over.

Most human nudists practiced as a way to connect with nature and feel more confident in themselves; their practice was not sexual in any way, and in fact, most human nudists had strict rules prohibiting any sexualized conduct in their spaces.

Galaxy View Resort was not like human nudist spaces.

Consent was non-negotiable, and everyone who came here had to sign the very strict behavioral policy. They were a zero-tolerance space for any questionable behavior. However, they were also up-front about the fact that looking and being looked at were a part of the gig. It was part vacation, part sex club.

Stella finally arrived at her destination after what felt like the longest walk of her life.

The spa was beautiful and surprisingly very different from the loud neons she had been immersed in since she boarded the station. It was dark green, all beautiful marble with veins of shimmery gold. Warm, textured tiles covered the ground, and despite the humidity of the space, she didn't feel like she would slip. There was a large, steamy hot tub in the center of the space, surrounded by elegant lounge chairs with soft, glowing lights beneath them. Some appeared to be salt chairs, while others were smooth stone. Several pathways led away from the main area, each with a sign indicating what portion of the spa it led to. On the far side of the space, there was a bar of sorts–though it didn't appear to have alcohol or any of the similar alien stimulants that were common these days. There were baskets of exotic fruit on shelves behind the bar, along with things you might find in ... smoothies. Stella could go for a smoothie, she thought, as she scanned the area again, deciding which seat to take.

There were only a few other people here, so Stella's task was thankfully low-stress. She decided on a lounger in the far corner of the main area–no one seemed to be sitting near there.

She made her way over and set her tote bag down next to the chair. There was a small side table, and she placed her phone and water bottle on it. She noticed a shelf of neatly rolled, plush towels nearby and stepped over to grab a few, laying one out on her chair. As she moved to adjust the top corner of the towel that had wadded up on itself, her elbow hit her metal water bottle. She gasped and tried to catch it, but it clattered to the ground with the loudest, most horrific clang Stella had ever heard.

The few people in the hot tub turned to look, and Stella whispered, "Sorry!" putting her hands up in front of her. She didn't wait to see their reactions before she turned and bent to pick it up from the ground. It occurred to her, devastatingly enough, that she was naked as she bent over, and was consequently flashing the entire room with a very explicit view.

A throat cleared behind her, and Stella wondered if there was some space balcony in this place she could launch herself off of.

"Can I get you anything?" The voice was melodic and feminine, with an accent Stella couldn't immediately place. She decided that staying bent over would only make this interaction worse, so she righted herself, water bottle in hand, as she began to answer.

"Oh, I think I'm..." she trailed off as she turned to face the speaker. Holy hell, this alien was beautiful.

They were Sozarin, their glittering skin an ethereal shade of electric lavender. They had striking ridges of dark purple on their high cheekbones, and their eyebrows and lashes were the same shade. Their eyes were multicolored, shades of blue, magenta, and purple, like a little galaxy contained in their irises. They stood about a foot taller than Stella ... and she was gawking up at them.

"Do you have smoothies here?" she asked absently. She could salvage this, maybe.

She tried to force herself to focus.

"Yes, we can make pretty much anything you like. Do you have any favorites?" The Sozarin regarded Stella as they spoke, and Stella felt even more exposed under their gaze.

"Oh, well, I like cherries," Stella said, blinking. The Sozarin was naked too—it had just hit Stella, and she fought to keep her gaze from drifting from the alien's perfect face.

"Alright, I'll see what I can mix up. Any allergies or anything I should be aware of?" The Sozarin seemed to be trying not to smile now. Stella could feel herself blushing.

"Ah, yes, I'm allergic to nuts."

"Noted. I'll be right back with your smoothie. I'm Zina, by the way. I use she/her. I'll be around this evening if you need anything at all while you're here."

Stella nodded and smiled. "I'm Stella, she/her." A thrill ran through Stella as she settled into her lounge chair—it was heated, and felt incredible against her bare skin. *Zina.* What a beautiful name for a beautiful being. It then occurred to Stella that she had introduced herself to her waitress, which was a super weird thing to do. Good grief. She took a deep breath and tried to collect herself before her Sozarin returned.

chapter two

Zina watched the little human from behind the counter as she worked. Zina felt bad for embarrassing her right after she'd dropped her water bottle–she hadn't meant to make her uncomfortable, but she obviously had. Stars, but she was pretty when she blushed. Zina had been working at the resort for a few months already, and the nudity didn't really affect her much. Not until now, anyway.

She had taken this job when her best friend, Reki, had finally worn her down. She could remember the conversation with them–they'd been bothering her for months to come to the station. The pay was good, and she'd been trying to save up to move off-world for years. Bartending at a resort wasn't the most glamorous job, and it certainly didn't put her degree to use, but she got to the point that she couldn't argue with the money. She knew this wouldn't be forever, but it was nice at least to spend more time with Reki.

Zina scooped some fresh chopped cherries into her blender cup and tried to focus. What went best with cherries ...

When she was satisfied with her cherry-lime-honey concoction, she added ice and blended it until smooth. She poured it into a pretty glass and popped a wide glass straw into it before heading back across the room to where the little human–Stella–sat.

Zina tried to keep her eyes fixed squarely on Stella's face, but as she approached, she couldn't help herself from stealing a glance at the human's smooth, rounded hip. The angle of the lounger cradled her lush body perfectly. Zina chided herself internally.

"One cherry-forward smoothie. Let me know if you don't like it, I'm happy to try something else," Zina said, bending to place the smoothie on the little end table. Stella turned to look up at her with a smile, and Zina felt a rush of warmth through her entire body.

"Thank you, Zina, I'm sure it will be delicious," Stella said, and took a sip.

Zina felt a disproportionate amount of pride–and also something else–as Stella moaned slightly.

"It's perfect," Stella said. She had dark brown hair that curled tightly; a few ringlets of it had escaped her bun and coiled at the nape of her neck in the humidity.

Zina realized she was staring. "Can I get you anything else?" She asked hastily.

"I'm all set, thank you!" Stella said, and the slight blush on her pretty, round cheeks didn't escape Zina's notice. That strange heat flared through Zina's body again, and this time the ridges on her cheekbones began to ache slightly. The ones on her arms and legs soon began to throb as well. Stars, this was not the time for her to be having some kind of allergic reaction. Her shift was only halfway over.

She returned to her station behind the counter and tidied up, wondering what she had touched that could be causing her to feel so strangely. That had to be it, right? Sozarins didn't catch colds or fevers like other species, but they did tend to have strange sensitivities. She'd worked with all these ingredients before, though, and nothing had bothered her ...

Most of the time, she was grateful for her life experiences–growing up with her adopted family on Moratu had given her a much broader picture of the galaxy than she would have had on Sozar. She loved her parents, and she was grateful for them, but times like this made her wish she had grown up around at least a few other Sozarins. She had read about some of the differences between Sozarins and Moratari, but it had been a long time. She pulled out her pocket console and did a quick search for any information on sudden allergic reactions in Sozarins, but before she could read anything helpful, a gaggle of patrons wandered up to the bar for smoothies.

She slipped on a pair of protective barrier bands this time; they rested just above her elbows and made a flexible shield between her skin and anything she touched.

Hopefully, that would keep her allergy at bay until she figured out what was going on.

Once that batch of drinks was finished, she cleaned her station and made a quick round, checking on anyone who had been seated for a while. Stella was still there, engrossed in a paper copy of a book, which Zina found quite adorable, actually. No one used paper books anymore.

Things seemed quiet, so she pulled her console back out and continued her search while rummaging through her work bag for an allergy pill. She hadn't really had an issue with allergies before, but she always kept a few with her just in case.

Everything she read confirmed what she already knew—Sozarin's allergies and intolerances were from birth, not developed later in life. Zina let out a huffy sigh of frustration. This was the last thing she needed in the middle of the day. Her shifts here were long—she had signed up for doubles pretty much every day to get the extra hours.

Zina knew that moving off-world was expensive, and she wanted to set herself up to be comfortable and have a financial safety net. She wasn't quite sure yet where off-world she wanted to live, but she spent her evenings researching all the possibilities.

She glanced back at the human woman, Stella, and wondered if she lived on Earth. Many humans had moved to other places in the galaxy, so it wasn't a certainty. Zina had researched Earth extensively, and she thought it would be amazing to visit at the very least. Everything there was so lovely and green.

Her eyes drifted back to Stella, and the throbbing itchiness on her ridges flared. Stars help her. This was awful. She knew there was another Sozarin on the staff at the resort–they were a concierge. She had been in onboarding training with them. She decided that she needed to have a little chat with them; they'd grown up on Sozar. Maybe they would know what in Stars' name was wrong with her.

chapter three

After an hour of reading by the hot tub, Stella finally felt a bit more relaxed. This had been a good idea–something about people being naked at the spa was less jarring than a stand-up comedy show would have been. She paused her reading to scan the room; there seemed to be a few people there on their own, but the thought of trying to talk to anyone was daunting.

She took a sip of her smoothie and glanced over to the bar area where that Sozarin–Zina–was wiping down the counter. Zina looked up to catch Stella staring, and she could feel the flush starting in her cheeks and spreading down her neck. Why was she like this?

A shuffling of footsteps pulled her attention toward the main entrance, and she looked up to see her friends coming in. She smiled and waved to them. Marie caught sight of her and elbowed Lenny, pointing. They all smiled and headed toward her.

Stella was glad to see them–this trip was obviously stressful for her for a few glaring reasons, but she was grateful for the time with her friends. She loved them–they were her family.

Dana dropped her bag down in the lounger next to Stella's. "So, seems like a nice spot you found, huh?"

"Yeah, this is so pretty! And like, super different vibes from the rest of the resort." Marie added, plopping down across from them.

"How was dinner?" Stella asked. She was trying to ignore how weird it was to be sitting here chit-chatting with her friends while they were all naked.

"Delish, and the comedy was great, too! The comedian was Troza, though, so a few of the jokes didn't make sense to us, but everyone else was eating it up!" Lenny said.

"I'm glad to hear!" Stella said. Each of her friends was so beautiful in their own way–Lenny with her dark skin and graceful, willowy limbs; Lenny with her rounded curves, smooth skin, and glossy black hair; Marie with her dark curls and thick eyelashes. It occurred to Stella that they'd said they'd be meeting up with Taylor for dinner, but ...

"Where did Taylor go?" Dana asked, interrupting Stella's thoughts.

"They went to the bathroom," Lenny answered.

"They're here now," Marie added, pointing over toward the bar. They all turned to look, and sure enough, Taylor was there ordering a drink.

"Hey, so that bartender is like the prettiest person I've ever seen," Lenny said, sounding almost concerned.

"Uh, yeah, agreed. You think Taylor is trying to hit on them?" Dana asked with a wry smile.

Taylor was leaning against the bar, their plump rear facing them. Their cropped blonde hair caught the glowy golden light of the spa, making it almost luminescent.

"Taylor can pull, though the bartender isn't their usual type," Marie observed.

This conversation, Stella realized, was making her feel something, though she couldn't quite place what just yet.

"She introduced herself to me when I sat down. Her name is Zina." Stella said, and Dana raised her eyebrows.

"She introduced herself, huh?"

"I mean, she took my order," Stella said in a hurry, holding up her smoothie.

"Uh-huh," Lenny said, a knowing look in her eyes.

Stella knew she was blushing again, and there was nothing to do to hide it. She looked over to the bar again, but this time Zina was looking right at her. Stella pulled in a silent breath and looked away.

"We will see, I guess. Taylor usually goes for more cutesy types, though." Lenny said.

"Yeah, cutesy like Marie," Dana added with a sly laugh.

"Oh my god," Marie said, rolling her eyes. "It was one time!"

They all looked up as Taylor walked over to join them, a bright blue drink in their hand.

"Stella, good to see you!" They said, giving Stella a warm smile. "It's been way too long. Crazy that it took going to space to get us all together at the same time."

Stella laughed at that–they were notoriously difficult to schedule as a group, but when they did get together, it felt like no time had passed at all.

"Hello there," a new voice spoke from Stella's left. "I'm Zina, and I'll be taking care of you this evening. Can I get anyone a smoothie or something else to drink?"

Lenny looked over at Stella and widened her eyes, urging her to do something. Stella wasn't sure exactly what Lenny had in mind–did she want Stella to jump the waitress right then and there? She shook her head slightly at Lenny, silently begging her to leave it alone.

"I'd love a smoothie!" Marie chimed in. "Dealer's choice," she added with a smile.

"Make that two," Dana said.

Lenny shook her head, "I'm all set, thanks!"

"Can I get you another?" Zina asked, looking at Stella.

"Oh! Um, yes, please. It was really good!" Stella looked up into Zina's strange galaxy eyes as she spoke, and Zina smiled at her, seeming genuinely pleased.

"Be right back," Zina said, and turned to go. Stella couldn't help herself from staring after Zina–her glittery skin caught the light as she moved, and holy shit, her ass was perfect. It was strange to see a tail up at the base of her spine–it curled lazily in the air behind Zina as she walked.

"Sooo, what's on the agenda tomorrow, Lenny?" Marie asked. Stella was still zoned out, watching Zina walk away and hoping absently that none of her friends noticed.

"Ok, so! We should for sure hit up the Boozy Beach Brunch in the morning, and then I figured we could have some free time in the afternoon to explore the resort or do whatever we want. I might nap. And then tomorrow night, I got us tickets to the Float Under the Stars party."

"Oh, what's that?!" Taylor asked before taking a sip of their drink.

"The party? So everyone gets an innertube or floaty of choice, and they dim the lights in the main pool area so you can look out the glass ceiling and see the stars!" Lenny answered.

Stella thought that sounded incredible, and she actually felt really excited about part of this trip. Maybe it wouldn't be all stressful.

"So, Stella," Dana said, and Stella felt the tiniest bit of dread at the expectant tone of Dana's voice. "What type of partner are you looking for? We should know so we can keep an eye out and help you."

"Yeah, we need to be your wingmen!" Marie added. They all looked at her, waiting.

"Well," Stella said, scrambling to find the right words in her mind. "I think I'm interested in women." Taylor nodded, and Dana chimed in with a supportive, "Ok!"

They all were still looking at her, waiting for her to say more.

"I guess someone with a nice butt?" She said hesitantly. They nodded, obviously wanting more details. "Someone...nice?" Lenny frowned a bit.

"I don't know what you all want me to say, she doesn't have to be my dream girl just for me to fuck her!" Stella said, a bit exasperated.

Her friends' eyes darted over to her left, and Stella knew before she even looked that Zina had approached with their drinks. She wanted to crawl into a hole somewhere and never be seen again.

"Ok, here are the two specials," Zina said, handing two glasses filled with pretty lavender drinks over to Marie and Dana. "And another cherry honey lime," she finished, setting the third glass on Stella's end table.

"Thank you!" Marie said, and Dana raised her glass to Zina, nodding her thanks.

Zina walked away, and Taylor choked out a laugh. "I bet she hears stuff like that all the time," they said, giving Stella's knee a friendly pat.

Stella risked a glance at the bar, and sure enough, Zina was looking back at her. Stella thought she saw just the hint of a smile on Zina's perfect lips.

chapter four

Zina had been a bit itchy all night, but it had at least gotten a bit better when she went back to her room in the staff wing of the resort. She had sent a text to her Sozarin friend on the station, asking if they had some time to chat soon, and had promptly collapsed into bed. Those double shifts could really take their toll.

The next morning, it was time, once again, to go clock in. She worked the morning shift at the main pool area. Those hours always seemed to go faster than the afternoons in the spa.

The soft soles of the sandals Zina wore barely made any noise on the lacquered neon floor as she made her way to the bar. Her shift started halfway through brunch, so not terribly early, but her time at the spa always stretched late into the evenings.

She arrived at the main hub of activity on the station; the lush tropical plants surrounding the main pool area came from many different planets, all interspersed here to form a rather breathtaking menagerie. The glass dome above showed the stars outside, the sight dimmed by the artificial sunlight that filled the room. Tonight was one of Zina's favorite things about working at the resort, though–they dimmed the lights to let the stars shine while people floated in the pool below. They did it once a week, but this time Zina had requested the evening off work so she could join in the fun.

Zina got to her home base for the morning right on time and was thrilled to see that Reki was there.

"Am I stuck with you today?" Zina asked as she approached. The bar was inside a small open-air restaurant right on the beach.

"Wouldn't you like to know?" Reki retorted with feigned annoyance. Zina laughed, stepping behind the bar. "But yes, you are stuck with me."

"This is amazing news. We have shit to catch up on." Zina said.

"Do we? What did you do this time?" Reki asked, and Zina smacked them lightly on the arm. Reki was Moratari, so very green and very buff. They had a humanoid torso but, instead of legs, lower bodies similar to those of a serpent. A light smack on the arm did, unfortunately, hurt Zina's hand, and she hissed, pulling it back to massage it lightly.

"That's what you get for hitting me," Reki said, lips pursed in mock sadness. Zina rolled her eyes.

"Ok, well first of all, I didn't do anything," Zina said, and Reki narrowed their eyes at her in disbelief.

"Uh-huh," they said.

"I didn't! I was just working my shift at the spa yesterday, and all of a sudden, all my ridges got so itchy and started kind of hurting. It was super weird."

"Do they still hurt?" Reki asked.

"A bit, yes. And they are definitely still itchy," she said, scratching at one of the ridges on her forearm.

"Well, what happened directly before you noticed it starting?" Reki asked. They always wanted to help their friends get to the bottom of things; it was one of the many things Zina loved about them.

"That's the weirdest part, it was just in the middle of my shift yesterday over at the spa. I'd been making smoothies all afternoon, I didn't touch anything weird, nothing changed really ... I noticed it after I went to take a human woman's order."

Reki paused, considering Zina's words, obviously trying to make sense of it just as Zina had been since it happened. Zina sighed heavily and turned to look out at the beach area that sprawled out beyond the awning of the little restaurant. Stella and the group of friends she had been with yesterday were staking their claim on one of the clusters of beach chairs, setting bags down and spreading towels out as they chatted.

"Actually, that's her over there," Zina said, gesturing with a jerk of her head. Reki looked up and studied the group.

"Which one?" they asked.

The prettiest one, Zina thought, but managed to keep herself from saying that bit out loud. "The shorter one with the long, dark brown curly hair and the," Zina trailed off.

"The incredible body?" Reki asked with a smile, glancing sidelong at Zina. "Is that what you were going to say? Because fuck me, she's stunning."

It wasn't unusual for Reki to say something to Zina when they saw a guest they found attractive, but for some reason, Zina felt a flash of anger at their words. Her ridges gave an uncomfortable throb.

"So, after you talked to her, is when you noticed the itching?" Reki continued.

"Yeah. Honestly, the whole thing was so weird. I freaked out last night and sent a message to Pazin," Zina said, forcing her bizarre anger to the back of her mind.

"Oh yeah? That's the Sozarin that was in orientation with you, right? They seem nice." Reki began pulling out tubs of garnishes to refresh the tiny bowls they kept on the counter for easy access.

"Mhm, they didn't get back to me yet, but I'm hoping maybe there's some secret Sozarin info that will make this make sense. You know I love my family, but they didn't exactly teach me about the intricacies of my species." Zina laughed and grabbed the cleaning supplies, wiping down the counter.

"Well, keep me posted, and let me know if there's

anything I can do to help you. I'm sorry you're not feeling great." Reki said, concern written on their face.

"Thanks," Zina smiled at her friend, and they fell into companionable silence as they prepped for the second wave of brunch-goers.

Zina was so caught up in the rhythm of working alongside Reki that she didn't notice Stella approaching the bar until she was seated on a stool in front of her.

"Hello again," Stella said, and Zina thought her voice was the most lovely sound she'd ever heard. She chided herself for being ridiculous and cleared her throat.

"Hi there, what can I get for you?" Zina said, trying to sound professional and aloof.

"Do you guys make Bellini's here?" Stella asked.

"That's ... champagne and peach juice, right?" Zina asked. Stella nodded.

Zina thought for a moment. "Hmm ... we don't have any peaches, but I think I have something that will be similar! Want to give it a go?"

"Yes, please. I need a drink if I'm going to be able to do this," Stella said with a nervous laugh.

"What are you trying to do?" Zina asked as she popped open a bottle of champagne. The smell of the stuff was so interesting to her, no matter how many times she experienced it.

"Flirt," said Stella with a groan.

"Ah," Zina said, pouring some of the bubbly golden liquid into a tall, thin glass.

As she poured, a muscled Troza walked up to the bar

and leaned against it right next to Stella. They glanced over at her appreciatively.

"Is it your first time visiting Galaxy View?" Their question was directed at Stella, who hadn't even looked in their direction prior to them speaking. Their voice was high-pitched and lilted with a heavy accent.

Stella turned to take in the Troza, and it was all Zina could do to keep making the drink. The Troza was objectively attractive; humanoid with leanly muscled arms and wide expanses of blue, marbled skin that looked like stone. They were a sculpture come to life.

"Yeah, my friends dragged me here for my birthday trip this year," Stella said with a laugh.

"Dragged you? You weren't too keen on coming, then?" The Troza shifted so their large breasts weren't hidden from Stella's view by their arms. Zina's ridges began to itch uncontrollably, but she resisted the urge to touch any of them.

"I, uh..." Stella's eyes darted down to take in the Troza's body.

"I'm Ilona, by the way," the Troza cut in. "I use she/her."

Stella's posture relaxed slightly. "I'm Stella, also she/her."

"So are you enjoying your time here, even if you were a bit unwilling?" Ilona asked.

"Yeah, it's really beautiful here." Stella still seemed anxious, and Zina wished there was something she could do.

"That it is," Ilona said, pausing to leave Stella room to ask her a question and keep the conversation going.

Stella stayed silent.

Zina finished her approximation of a Bellini and set it in front of Stella, who took it, thanked Zina, and met her gaze with a hint of panic. Zina glanced over at Ilona, who seemed like she was about to try to talk to Stella again.

"What can I get started for you?" Zina asked, and Ilona's eyes cut to hers.

"Oh! Right. Could I please have a Moratari sunrise?"

Zina nodded and began to make the drink. When it looked like Ilona might talk to Stella again, Zina said, "Visiting for long?"

Ilona looked at Zina, just the barest hint of frustration on her face. "Not this time around; just a few days," Ilona answered with finality.

Zina wasn't about to let it go, though. For some reason, she felt compelled to help Stella; it was obvious she was uncomfortable talking to Ilona.

"Ah, a regular, then? Do you come often?" Zina asked, giving the cocktail a shake before pouring it into a heavy, low-walled glass.

"Occasionally," Ilona answered, not smiling this time.

"Here you go! You just let us know if there's anything else we can get you." Zina gave Ilona her best customer service smile. Ilona took the drink, glanced at Stella–who was pointedly looking in the opposite direction, and walked away.

Stella didn't immediately say anything, so Zina gave her a moment, tidying up from making those two drinks. After a long moment, she ventured, "So … that was awkward, huh?"

Stella looked at her with pleading green eyes–Zina imagined that must be the color of all the trees on Earth.

"Yeah, it was." Stella sounded defeated. "It's just … I'm so bad at this. That Troza was hot, but I didn't know what to say? Like, yeah, I'm here for my birthday, and it's nice to spend time with my friends, but they brought me here to get laid for the first time, and it just feels like a lot of pressure, and I'm afraid I'm going to say something super weird, you know?" Stella froze for a moment before slapping her hand over her mouth.

Zina suppressed her smile.

"Weird like that," Stella whispered. She was blushing, and Zina thought it was adorable.

"That's not weird," Zina said with a wave of her hand, trying to put Stella at ease.

"I'm almost thirty, and I've never had sex with anyone … back on Earth, people might give me a hard time about that. Also, going on a birthday trip for the express purpose of finding someone to fuck?" Stella looked at Zina incredulously.

"People come here to see the escorts all the time," Zina said casually.

"Yeah, but … I really wanted to try to find someone who maybe wanted to do that with me for fun." Stella's voice was quieter now. Stars, she was pretty. Zina's eyes roved over her bare skin, each gentle roll of her stomach, the way the softness of her upper arms pressed her tits together ...

She was staring again.

"Right, ok, so you want to do this the old-fashioned way, but you're feeling too pressured?" Zina asked.

"Yeah, like just now, I know my friends are back there watching," Stella gestured behind her without turning around. "I know they're going to ask me a million questions when I go back over there. I just feel like there's not enough time and not enough space and..." she trailed off, running her fingers through her dark curls. "Ugh."

"You think it would be less overwhelming to find what you're looking for if your friends weren't on your case?" Zina asked. Even she wasn't quite certain what the purpose of her question was.

"Yeah, I mean, I think that would help for sure. I just don't do well when people ask me a million questions and try to help. It makes me freeze. Case in point." Stella gestured to where Ilona had been standing.

Zina felt faintly nauseous thinking about Stella sleeping with someone else. Before Zina could fully form the thought, words started coming out of her mouth. "Maybe I can help? Keep them off your back a bit?"

"How ... would you do that?" Stella asked, downing the last of her drink.

"You could tell them that we fucked," Zina said with a shrug.

Stella choked on her Bellini.

"What?!"

"You could just tell them that we did it, and then they'll think it already happened and leave you alone enough that maybe you can actually find what you're looking for with someone without them all in your business." Zina had no idea what had possessed her to propose this–why did she feel such a need to help this random human woman?

"Why would you help me like that?" Stella asked, confused.

"Could be fun," Zina said with a wink. Stars, what had gotten into her?

Reki hustled back behind the counter, then, arms full of packages of napkins. Zina also noticed a few of Stella's friends heading toward the bar.

Stella tracked Zina's gaze and turned to look at what had caught her attention. She turned back around, eyes wide, and stared at Zina.

When one of her friends sidled up to her at the bar, Stella quickly said, "So I'll see you when your shift is over, then?"

Zina couldn't believe what she was hearing.

"Yeah, I'll take you to get ice cream," Zina said slowly, smiling. Stella's friend, the one with pink tips at the end of her long black hair, opened her mouth in surprise, eyes wide in delight.

"Stella!" she exclaimed.

"Lenny! This Bellini was fire, you should get one." Stella sounded a bit breathless, and her cheeks were rosy.

Zina smiled. She had herself a date with Stella—even if it was just a fake one.

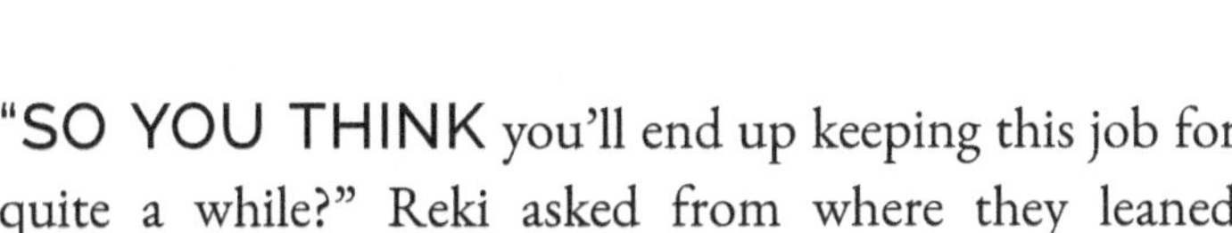

"SO YOU THINK you'll end up keeping this job for quite a while?" Reki asked from where they leaned against the counter next to Zina.

"What? No, you know I don't really like it here, why would you ask me that?" Zina was affronted—her best friend knew very well why she'd taken this job, and it was one hundred percent about the paycheck. She didn't want to be here long.

"Well, it just seemed like maybe you were getting a bit more settled if you're willing to, uh ... go on dates with the clients?" Reki was trying hard not to smile, and Zina rolled her eyes.

"It's not what you think, Reki."

"Isn't it? You never do anything but go back to your room to rest after your double shifts, but I just heard you make plans with that human. The same one, if I'm not mistaken, that made you so itchy yesterday?"

At Reki's words, her ridges flared again as if they could hear the mention of their plight. "She didn't *make* me itchy, it was just a coincidence."

"Uh huh." Reki gave her side eye as she reached to put some bananas away.

"I told her I'd help her keep her friends off her case, that's all," Zina said with a small shake of her head. Even if she would do something more with Stella, she hadn't seemed interested in that. Zina just wanted to help however she could.

"Right, so you're going on a pretend date with a super hot woman, and it's just a favor to her?" Reki asked.

"Right," Zina answered, her eyebrows raised, daring Reki to contradict her.

"Ok, Z. I hope you two have lots of pretend fun together."

Zina's console buzzed—it was time to head to the spa.

"See you later, Reki," Zina said, waving to her friend.

"Yeah, I'll see you at the party tonight," Reki responded, and Zina made her way across the resort to the spa. This was about to be the longest afternoon of her life.

chapter five

"**O**h my GOD, Stella!!!" Marie squealed when Lenny had finished announcing that Stella would be going on a date with "that super hot bartender from the spa".

"Hell yeah, I knew she could pull," Dana said with a smile, elbowing Stella gently.

"What are you guys going to do?" Taylor asked.

"Ice cream," Stella said. The rush of adrenaline she'd had when she agreed to Zina's plan hadn't completely died down.

"Ok, that's cute! Are you going to invite her back to your room after … ?" Marie trailed off, eyebrows raised.

"Fingers crossed!" Stella said with an anxious laugh. She had to make it seem real so she could have some breathing room to maybe find someone to hook up with on her terms.

"You still have time for facials?" Lenny asked,

pointing over her shoulder toward the doors to the main spa at the resort.

"Oh, yeah, totally!" Stella said, nodding. She was so relieved they'd be doing a mostly quiet activity between now and the time she was supposed to meet back up with Zina.

"Amazing!" Lenny said, clapping her hands together. "Ok, our appointments start in like thirty, so let's make sure we are done with brunch stuff in a few, so we can head over there."

The group nodded and turned back to their plates. Suddenly, the pancakes Stella had ordered seemed like a lot. She took a few bites, but her nerves were still too much to really eat. She decided just to get a snack at the spa–they always had fruit and stuff at places like that.

Stella risked a glance over at the bar, and she saw Zina leaning over it to hand a drink to a customer. Her perfect tits pressed against the edge of the counter, and the line of her back from this angle was ... so perfectly muscled and beautiful. Stella's mouth went a bit dry.

"Come on, we are going to be late!" Lenny's voice snapped Stella back into the present. She grabbed her tote bag and followed her friends. The fact that they were all naked would hit her every now and again, and it did then as they were walking. Stella laughed a bit at the ridiculousness of it all.

Once they were inside the main spa–a much more imposing space than the one where she'd first met Zina–they all split up, following their estheticians to their stations. Stella gaped at the space as she walked. It was all crystal clear glass; the roof of the massive main room offered a perfect view of the stars outside. Pools dotted the expansive lobby, some steaming and others obviously very cold, based on the expressions of the people in them. The service rooms were all mirrored on the outside to provide a private experience without detracting from the lobby's glassy openness.

Stella's esthetician was a human; she had on an apron, which Stella supposed made sense given her role here. She suddenly wondered if the cooks were allowed to wear clothes.

"Alright, tell me a bit about your skin. Do you tend to run dry or oily?" The esthetician walked Stella through a number of similar questions before nodding and turning to prepare products for the facial. Stella lay back on the cot and took a deep breath, trying to relax. All she could think about, though, was what it would be like to go on a fake date with Zina.

She played different versions of what could happen in her mind, each more distressing than the last. In one version, she dropped her ice cream all over herself and had to wipe sticky ice cream off her bare chest. She knew that would be overstimulating to her—to be so sticky like that—and she would have to leave to rinse off. In another version of events, she imagined herself accidentally saying something incredibly offensive to Zina. In this scenario, Zina would storm off in a rage, and Stella would want to die.

Stella always did this—got in her own head about all the ways something could go wrong. Sometimes she thought about the ways that something could go right, too, but if she let herself fixate on that too much, she would end up disappointed when that didn't become reality.

She sighed as the esthetician began gently painting on a cool gel. It felt nice, and Stella tried to fix her focus on the sensations in her body.

Whatever she did must have worked because she woke with a start as her esthetician said, "Ok Stella, you're all set." Stella tried to play it off, sitting up promptly and attempting to seem very much alert and awake.

"Thank you so much," Stella said with a smile as she slipped off the cot.

"The redness shouldn't last too long, it's just a natural side effect of some of the resurfacing work we did."

Stella's heart dropped. Redness? Oh god, how bad was it? As she followed the esthetician out, she turned to catch a glimpse of herself in the mirrored wall, and she nearly fell over. Her face and neck were *bright* red. Fuck.

Marie and Taylor were already done, waiting in some of the lounge chairs near the entrance to the spa. As Stella approached, Marie caught sight of her and put her hand over her mouth. Fuck, it was really that bad.

Taylor noticed Marie's expression and started to ask

her what was wrong, but they looked over their shoulder as they spoke and froze when they saw Stella.

"Aw, man," Taylor whispered.

"Yeah, so, I think it's pretty bad, huh?" Stella said, plopping down in a chair next to them. "She said it would go away soon, but..."

"But you're about to go on your date!" Marie said, her brows furrowed in concern.

"Yeah. I am." Stella pulled her water bottle from her bag and took a long drink. She knew it wasn't a real date, but Stella still didn't want to look heinous for it. Even though it was fake, Zina was hot, and Stella weirdly wanted to impress her.

"Does this happen every time you get a facial?" Taylor asked.

"Well, I don't really get facials. But it did happen once when I was a teenager; I just assumed the gal that did it used the wrong stuff on me."

"How fast did it go away that time?" Marie asked.

"It took a few hours, I think?" Stella leaned back in her chair, crossing her legs.

"Ok, that's not so bad." Taylor was trying to sound encouraging.

"Yeah, not terrible." Marie put her hand on Stella's. Stella just nodded. She wanted to go back to her room more than anything, but she was the one who had agreed to Zina's plan. She couldn't very well bail on it now.

"I'm just going to go over to the ice cream place. Wish me luck!" Stella said, standing. She hustled out of the spa before Marie or Taylor could protest. She knew it would have been nice to wait for Lenny and Dana, but she was already anxious. Hearing two more people comment about how red her face was definitely wasn't going to help her.

As she walked, she dug one of her ginger hard candies from her bag. They often helped her anxiety, and she thought now was as good a time for one as any.

By the time she had crossed the massive central atrium of the resort, the hard candy had nearly dissolved. Walking around this place naked was starting to feel less weird; she had almost forgotten about it completely that time.

The little ice cream shop was decorated all in pastels, with giant rainbow sprinkles on the storefront. The tiles covering the shop floor also had a sprinkled pattern, and a long counter made of ice cream coolers ran the length of the shop. There was a scattering of little tables and chairs around, but the shop was thankfully almost empty. Stella hoped it would last.

She stepped further inside and noticed Zina sitting at the table all the way in the back corner. She looked up at Stella almost immediately, smiling and offering her a little wave. Stella took a breath and made her way over.

Zina stood as she approached, and holy shit, she was tall. Stella had noticed it before, but she'd never stood this close to Zina. Stella barely came up to her shoulder.

She tipped her head back a bit to look up at Zina, who smiled down at her. "It's good to see you again, Stella." If Stella's face wasn't already red from the facial, she knew it would have been flushing now.

"You too, Zina." Zina gestured to the table and pulled out a chair for Stella.

"Thanks," Stella said quietly, taking the offered seat.

"So..." Zina said with an almost mischievous smile.

"So," Stella laughed awkwardly.

"What made you decide to take me up on my weird offer to fake a hook-up?"

The bluntness of Zina's question took Stella by surprise, and she let out a real laugh this time. "I panicked." She decided to be honest rather than make up a clever response.

"Fair enough, I think I would have too if I'd been you," Zina said. A waiter came over to their table then, a small notepad in hand.

"You two know what you'd like?" they asked.

Zina looked to Stella. "Ready to order, or do you want to look at a menu for a minute?"

"I'm ready; I'd just like a scoop of vanilla, please." Stella smiled at the waiter.

"I'll have a strawberry milkshake, please," Zina said. The waiter nodded and headed back behind the counter.

"Strawberry, huh? You like Earth fruit?" Stella asked.

"I do! It's one of my favorites, actually." Zina shifted in her chair, and Stella was transfixed by the way her hair moved and how the light caught the shimmer of her skin.

"Have you been to Earth?" Stella was grateful they

had fallen right into a conversation that did not involve how red her face was.

"I haven't yet, but I'd really like to go! I took this job to save up so I can hopefully move off-world someday." Zina glanced out the window into the atrium before giving Stella a warm smile.

"I see. That's a big move!" Stella was desperately trying to stay focused on the conversation, not on how absolutely wild she must look with her face so red.

"It is, but I've always wanted to do it. I grew up in an adopted family away from Sozar, which gave me a taste of what the rest of the universe could be like. I'd like to pick a nice place and maybe go to graduate school–maybe even have a family one day!"

Zina absolutely transfixed Stella; she spoke so openly and easily, seemed so settled in herself, even just in the first few minutes of their fake date.

"What about you, Stella? What are all of your hopes and dreams?" Zina's voice snapped Stella out of her almost hypnotic state. Her tone was light, with a touch of humor that made Stella feel at ease.

"Hmm ... well, I'd like to have a family too, build a home with someone. I've just been wrapped up in my job, and before that, school. I have amazing friends, so I don't often actively feel like there's stuff missing from my life, you know?" The waiter returned with their ice cream as Stella finished speaking, and she took a bite of hers. It was creamy, sweet, and comforting.

"What do you do for work?" Zina asked, bending forward slightly to take a sip of her milkshake.

"I'm a software engineer. I work for one of the big tech companies on Earth. I get to work from home, though, which I really enjoy!"

"Oh, that does sound nice," Zina said earnestly. "You must make your home really comfortable then?"

"I try to! I like cozy things, so there's lots of nice places to sit with blankets and these big squishy plushies I like, and I have a million different kinds of tea." Stella stopped herself, feeling a bit embarrassed at rambling. "I'm sorry, I know you're just doing this with me to be nice..."

Zina's ethereal purple brow furrowed slightly at Stella's words. For an alien, her expressions were startlingly similar to a human's.

"Stella, I wouldn't ask if I didn't want to know. We're here because I wanted to be nice, sure, but that doesn't mean we can't be friends."

Right. Be friends with the nicest, most beautiful, hottest person Stella had ever seen. She could do that. "Alright," was all she could manage, along with a nod and a nervous smile.

"So, now that we are going to 'fuck'," Zina gave an exaggerated wink, "you should have some space to get out there and find someone to actually fuck. You said you really don't want to work with an escort, though?"

Stella snorted a laugh at Zina's wink. "I mean, I will– I don't have anything against them. I know they're some of the best in the galaxy. I just was hoping maybe *some* sort of feeling might be involved, even if it is just surface-level interest or lust."

"I can understand that." Zina's voice was still kind, but her posture had tensed slightly in a way that Stella didn't quite understand. She took another bite of her ice cream in silence, staring out the window as she absently licked her spoon.

When she glanced back at Zina, her eyes were fixed on Stella's mouth. Stella cleared her throat, and Zina quickly looked away.

"Oh, also," Stella said after a long moment, "thank you for not saying anything about how red my face is. Was? It may have gone away by now. Anyway, thanks."

Zina laughed, and the sound was so pretty that Stella thought she might be staring with her mouth open.

"Well, that would have been rude. Plus, I figured you'd just been to the spa or something; it happens to a lot of the humans that come here." Zina sipped her milkshake again, and it made a slurping noise in the straw as the glass emptied. "It did go away, for the record."

"Well, that's a relief," Stella rolled her eyes and chuckled.

"Ok, so ... we had ice cream. Should we ... ?" Zina asked pointedly, her eyes shifting toward the door.

"Oh! Right, yeah. Do you ... want to come back to my room with me? To 'fuck'?" Stella made airquotes around her last word, and Zina laughed.

"Oh, absolutely."

Stella knew Zina was joking, but she sort of–maybe really–wished she wasn't.

chapter six

Stars help her. Zina knew this was all pretend, but she realized she absolutely would fuck this adorable human woman. She was easy to talk to and even easier to get lost in–her pretty pink tongue had transfixed Zina on her spoon. She wanted to feel that tongue on her–*NO. No,* she scolded herself. She couldn't offer to do something nice like this and then just be a pervert the whole time.

Zina followed Stella back to her room across the resort, desperately trying not to stare at her perfect curves. Her hips swayed as she walked, her perfect ass jiggling just a bit, and these incredible, soft rolls across her back ... Zina wanted to run her fingers across them, bite them.

What, in the name of all the Stars, had gotten into her? She was never like this. She'd felt sexual desire, sure, but she'd never been ... obsessed like she seemed to be with Stella.

Images flashed through Zina's mind of Stella's pretty face, her round, green eyes, her wild mane of dark curly hair. She was just so, so beautiful.

"Here we are!" Stella said, stepping up to a door near the end of the long hallway. Zina realized she had been completely zoned out; she hoped she hadn't missed anything Stella had said.

"You guys got the nice rooms, huh?" Zina said, stepping inside as Stella held open the door.

"Yeah, well, splurge for my birthday and all that. I can't get over the balcony, though! It's so cool to sit out there and watch the stars. I don't know how you don't do it constantly." Stella said, walking over to look out the glass door.

Zina looked around the room–it wasn't *that* different from the staff rooms–just bigger, mostly.

"Have you used the hot tub yet?" she asked, gesturing to the infinity pool in the corner of the space.

"Oh, no, I haven't yet! We just got in yesterday, and we had brunch this morning, so ... busy, you know?" Stella sounded just the slightest bit out of breath, and her cheeks were pink as she bustled around the room doing what seemed to Zina like nothing at all.

"We should probably stay in here for a bit to be convincing, right? We could hop in?" Zina suggested, stepping toward the hot tub.

"Hop in...the hot tub? Like together?" Stella asked, her eyes going a bit wide. "Oh! Yeah, totally, we can do that."

"Cool! I've never gotten to be in one of the guest rooms before; they're nice," Zina said, stepping into the warm, steamy water. She waited on the second stair for Stella to approach and offered her a hand as she stepped in. Every nerve in her body lit up when Stella's hand touched hers. A wave of heat as she'd never felt before washed over her, and she was fairly certain it was not from the hot tub.

"Oh, really? Is this like ... allowed? Fraternizing with the guests and all?" Stella asked, and all Zina could do was focus on what she was saying.

"Yeah, management doesn't mind as long as it doesn't affect our attendance," Zina said, still reeling at the feel of Stella's skin on hers.

"I have to say, being in my room naked with you is somehow even weirder than chatting naked at an ice cream shop," Stella said with a laugh.

Zina chuckled at that. "The whole idea is pretty funny to me still, to be honest. Some species prefer not to wear clothes, but Sozarins are not one of them."

"Well, I guess it depends for humans, but this human hasn't been naked this much since she was an infant." Stella rolled her eyes, and Zina realized she really *liked* Stella.

The heat that had started to subside after touching Stella's hand came rushing back full force, this time accompanied by possibly the most intense arousal Zina had ever experienced. It nearly took her breath away.

Her ridges were tingling, and she found herself unable to look away from Stella, who was looking down at the water in the hot tub with a surprised expression. What was she ...

"Oh, I didn't realize Sozarins had tentacles, that's amazing!"

Zina forced her eyes to follow where Stella was looking, and pure horror zapped through her at what she saw.

One of her vaginal tentacles, long and purple, was protruding from her slit beneath the surface of the water. Stars, this was the most embarrassing thing that had ever happened to her. Her tentacles had never come out before, for any reason! Was she dying? She decided she had to leave *immediately*.

"Oh! I'm actually not feeling the best. I think I should head out now," Zina said, struggling to her feet and clumsily exiting the hot tub. "Mind if I borrow a towel?" she asked, not waiting for Stella's response before grabbing one.

She heard Stella call after her as she stumbled out into the hallway, towel wrapped tightly around her chest. Her nudity at the resort had never bothered her, really, but the thought of having a tentacle on display was too much for her right now. She took a few deep breaths, trying to collect herself as she began to walk as briskly as she could toward the staff wing.

The sound of voices down the hall greeted her all too soon, though. Shit. It was Stella's friends. She would have to act casual. She rounded the corner and sure enough, there they were. They all looked at her but didn't attempt to stop her. She smirked at them and winked, but kept walking. Hopefully, that would be enough to help Stella out.

It felt like an eternity before Zina made it back to her room. She collapsed on her bed with a groan.

Her console made a pinging noise from where it rested on her nightstand. She reluctantly rolled over to look at it, and the name that appeared made her brow furrow in confusion.

It was her ex girlfriend, Priscilla? What in all the Stars could she possibly want?

Zina opened the message, her eyes quickly scanning its contents. Some nonsense about feeling that ending things had been a mistake and that she wanted to give things another chance. Zina had been the one to end that relationship, and it had certainly not been a mistake.

As she read, imagining being with Priscilla, she felt physically ill. Maybe she really was sick.

She lay back on her bed and closed her eyes, hoping that maybe she was just overtired. That had to be it.

ZINA WOKE with a start to the sound of a knock on her door.

Shit, she hadn't meant to fall asleep. She rose quickly, the towel from Stella's room still wrapped around her.

"Pazin!" She opened the door to the welcome sight of her Sozarin friend from orientation. "Oh, I'm so glad to see you," she said, not even trying to conceal her relief. She felt itchy again.

"Zina, greetings! I thought, based on your note, that it might be best to have a chat in person." Pazin gave her a friendly smile, which Zina returned, gesturing for them to step inside her room.

"So, what seems to be..." Pazin began, but Zina couldn't keep her mouth shut, interrupting them.

"Ok, so yesterday I started getting super itchy all over my ridges, and it kind of went away, but it comes back every so often. And then also I got like *really* grossed out a bit ago when my ex texted me, which was kind of weird, and there's this human woman that I met yesterday, and when I'm around her I feel like a little dizzy and also hot? And just now, I was with her and..." Zina leaned in and whispered, "*my tentacle came out!*"

She stopped then and looked at Pazin expectantly. Their eyebrows were raised, and their mouth was agape. "Does any of that sound like Sozarin stuff to you?"

Pazin looked like they were trying not to laugh. "It does, in fact."

"Really?! Oh, thank the Stars," Zina said.

"Your ridges appear to be glittering, which definitely explains the itchiness you've been experiencing. Congratulations are in order, my friend!" Pazin gave her a broad smile.

"Congratulations? What do you mean?" Zina had never been so confused in her life.

"Oh, well, you found your mate!" Pazin seemed confused at Zina's confusion.

"My WHAT?" Zina accidentally shouted a bit. "Pazin," she started, collecting herself, "you have to talk to me like I know nothing, because I don't. Please could you explain from the beginning?"

Pazin nodded slowly, looking just a touch frightened of her after her outburst.

"Sozarins' ridges respond biologically when we find our mate, the person we're meant to be with romantically. It's a complicated process, but basically they have a bioluminescent sparkle for the duration of your courtship."

Zina raised her fingers to graze one of the ridges on her face. "You mean ... I'm sparkly? To impress my ..."

"Your mate, yes." Pazin nodded.

"Ok ..." Zina tried to let this information sink in.

"That is also the reason you felt physical repulsion upon hearing from your former partner. Your body now only wants your mate. You may also have strong reactions if your mate is close to other possible partners." *Shit.*

"It's Stella." Zina rubbed her temples, her head beginning to throb.

"The human you mentioned? That does make sense!" Pazin added.

"What about the tentacle situation? I didn't think they were supposed to be...external." Zina's mind raced, trying to put together all of the pieces of the last day.

"Ah, yes! That's normal. They only protrude when one is having intercourse with a mate." Pazin made it sound so clinical, but the feelings Zina had felt as it happened had been the most overwhelming of her life.

"Ok, great. That's not overwhelming at all, just good to know, really." Zina said, coping with dry humor as she almost always did.

"This is wonderful news, Zina. Some Sozarins go their whole lives without finding their mates! You and your human are very lucky indeed." Pazin sounded truly happy for her, but Zina's head was spinning. Stella wouldn't want to *be* with her like that–for life. Stars, she'd just come here for a birthday vacation, not to find a life partner!

"Is there anything else I should know about?" Zina asked, looking up at Pazin from where she now sat on the edge of her bed.

"I ... don't think so," Pazin said cheerfully.

"Well, thank you for all the information. I'm grateful for my adopted family, but it's times like this I wish I had grown up on Sozar."

"Ah, yes, well, it's nothing you can't overcome. You'll learn!" Pazin smiled down at her. She must have looked as overwhelmed as she felt, because they nodded and turned to go. "I'll leave you be, my friend. Just send me a note if anything comes up. Oh, and I'd love to meet your mate whenever you feel ready for that sort of thing!"

Pazin left Zina's room then, closing the door softly behind them. Zina fell back on her bed and covered her face with her arms. She had no idea what to do.

chapter seven

It was strange to call things day and night when, really, it looked the same outside the station all the time. They had set the station to run on Trozul time, and it was fairly similar to Earth–it came out to about 26 Earth hours. The lights would come up in the "morning" and dim slowly in the "evening", though the station never truly slept. Various activities and dining options, along with common areas, were available to guests at any time.

The pool, however, was usually kept quite bright, Stella had noticed. That made it all the more striking when she followed her friends into the central atrium the night after Zina had made her ... hasty exit. That had left Stella with more confusing emotions than she knew what to do with, so she had taken a stress nap. When her friends had excitedly knocked on her door to go to the starlight pool party, she had considered telling them she didn't feel well. Now, she was so glad she hadn't.

The dome of the central atrium looked crystal clear, and the white light of the stars around them was so bright it reminded Stella of a full moon back on Earth. The space was intimately lighted with fairy lights strung around the greenery, floating in the water–some even drifted through the air, she noticed with a touch of awe. It was magical.

Almost magical enough to take her mind off how Zina had practically run away earlier.

Her friends had managed to keep from asking her about her date for the fifteen minutes they'd been together, but Marie couldn't keep it together any longer.

"I was going to play it cool, Stella, but you HAVE to tell us!" she said, turning suddenly to face Stella as the group was setting their bags down on a cluster of pool chairs.

Stella looked up at Marie, surprised by the outburst, and realized, in horror, that she had no idea what to tell her friends.

"Oh! Yeah, it was great!" She forced herself to smile.

"Uh-huh ..." Taylor urged her to continue.

"It was really fun, Zina's super nice. And we ... um," Stella trailed off.

"You guys fucked?!" Dana asked.

"Oh my god, they totally did," Lenny chimed in.

"Yeah! So that was great too!" Stella added quickly, eager not to have to say the words herself for some reason. She felt confused at her own emotions–pretending she had fucked Zina was the whole point.

This was the reason they'd gone through all this mess: to get her friends to give her some space. Now that she was here, though, and the lie was leaving her lips ... she felt disappointed somehow.

"Is that all you have to say? Stella, you fucked an alien!" Marie exclaimed.

"Ok, so for sure yell it for the whole resort to hear," Stella laughed anxiously. Why was she disappointed?

"Leave her alone, guys, she will tell us when she wants to. For now, congrats, Stella; it's super exciting, and I hope you had the best time," Dana said, sensing Stella's discomfort.

"I did, yeah!" Stella said brightly, glad the conversation seemed to be ending. "Should we get in?" Stella asked, gesturing to the pool. There were piles of various floaties around, and she began to move toward one. She wanted a noodle.

Her friends followed, excited to float and literally stare out into space.

The water was warm on Stella's legs as she waded into the pool. It was a magical experience–the glow of the tiny lights on the water, the expanse of the galaxy above.

She and her friends bobbed in the water, chatting and laughing about things they'd laughed about a million times before. Stella loved her friends more than anything, and times like this made her feel that affection deep in her bones. She was so caught up in listening to them talk and staring up at the stars that she didn't realize she'd drifted a bit. She felt the impact just as she heard a surprised voice behind her.

"Shit, I'm so sorry!" Stella nearly fell off her noodle in her haste to turn around and apologize.

She came face to face with a Troza–a particularly beautiful one.

The Troza's eyes drifted over Stella's body in a way that made her feel warm all over.

"It's perfectly alright, these things happen. What's your name?" The Troza's voice was a rich alto with no small amount of raspy vocal fry. The Troza were from a rocky planet, and their characteristics were also stone-like. This one had beautiful dark gray-blue skin that looked like polished granite.

"I'm Stella," she offered the alien a smile. "I use she/her. And you are?"

"Breta, she and they," the Troza extended a hand, which Stella shook.

"A human handshake, huh? I didn't know you all did that on Trozul."

"Well, there are lots of humans that come to Galaxy View, so I studied up a bit on customs before my trip. I find humans fascinating." Breta wasn't much taller than Stella, but she looked like she could easily heft Stella up over her shoulder. She had a lush, curvy, muscular body and broad shoulders. They were exactly the sort of person Stella would want to pursue. So why didn't she feel even a little bit excited about chatting with Breta?

"What about us do you find so interesting? I think

we're rather dull, compared to all of the other species out there." Stella said with a chuckle.

"I hear that humans–especially human women–are very sexually compatible with Troza." Breta's expression was open, inviting. Stella opened her mouth to reply, searching for something flirty to say–this was exactly the sort of opportunity she'd been wanting. Why couldn't she let herself do it?

The thought hit her then–it wasn't Zina. She wanted Zina.

Zina, who had run away earlier today, even from a date that wasn't real.

"Who would have thought! Well, I hope you enjoy your night, Breta. It was great meeting you, and sorry again for the collision." Stella felt her disappointment pulling her down. Why couldn't she let Zina go? She obviously had no actual interest in Stella. She needed to get over it.

She waded back over to her friends with her noodle, wrapped it behind her back, and sank into the water, letting it support her enough to keep her face above water. She silently grabbed Dana's hand to keep from floating away again and let herself get lost staring at the stars above.

Stella wasn't sure how long they were there, but it felt like a long time. At some point, Marie had started yawning, and they'd all agreed it was time to go to bed.

Stella's thoughts drifted back to Zina–the beautiful purple of her skin, its slight shimmer. Stella wondered if

Zina was as soft as she looked. She was muscular, but her skin was so smooth, and her curves ... she stopped herself. This wasn't helping anything.

"We don't have anything big planned tomorrow, right?" Taylor asked as they neared their rooms.

"Nope, nothing through the day. There's a party tomorrow night, though!" Lenny answered with just as much energy as she somehow always had.

"Night! Love you guys," Stella said, waving to them and slipping into the quiet of her room.

Her eyes immediately went to the hot tub, and she felt her disappointment flare again, tightening her throat. Images of Zina's body, dripping wet, that purple tentacle Stella had seen beneath the surface ... heat gathered between Stella's legs.

She shifted her hips, and the friction had her nipples hardening. She rolled her eyes at herself—she was hopeless.

She eventually wanted to go to sleep, so she hopped into the shower to rinse off, then wrapped herself in a massive plush towel. She went over to her suitcase and dug out her favorite vibrator before getting comfortable on her bed. She let herself think of Zina then, doing her best to quiet the voices of shame and rejection in her mind. She turned on her vibrator and took a deep breath, permitting herself to feel pleasure as she placed the opening against her clit.

Stella imagined what it would feel like to put her hands on Zina's perfect tits, pinching her nipples and kissing her graceful neck. She thought of what it might feel like for her chest to be pressed to Zina's, her hands tangled in Zina's thick purple hair. In her mind, Zina's tail wrapped around her leg, and Stella's fingers sought out the slit that she had been so careful not to stare at. She conjured Zina's moan in her mind, and pleasure spiked through her, tingling through her lower back.

She imagined Zina's fingers finding her own entrance, brushing so lightly, savoring the wetness there. She would smile at Stella and slip two fingers inside, stretching Stella around her, stroking that place inside ...

Stella came with a gasp, her inner walls clamping down desperately. She sighed as she came down from the high, switching off her vibrator. Fuck, she wanted Zina so badly. What a mess she'd managed to get herself into.

chapter eight

Zina had managed to keep her distance from Stella all night at the starlight pool party. It hadn't been easy, especially when that Troza had been flirting with her. She had done it, though, and she was exhausted, anxious, and confused.

She collapsed into bed, eager to get the night over with. Maybe tomorrow she would see Stella again, even if it was from far away.

Zina woke with a gasp to the sound of her last, final, it's-really-time-to-get-up-now alarm. She glanced at the time and cursed, rolling out of bed and gathering her hair into a ponytail as she stumbled to her mirror. Thankfully, there was no need to fuss with clothes here, but she still managed to look more frazzled than usual as she rushed out the door.

Reki was already behind the bar when Zina arrived. They had a smug look on their face until they took in Zina's disheveled state.

"Whoa, are you good?" they asked.

"Uh, debatable," Zina answered as she scanned the beach area for Stella or her friends, but she didn't see them.

"How was your 'date'?" Reki set down the glass they'd been drying, following Zina's gaze.

"Well, mostly it was really good, but then really bad?" Zina said, not sure where to even start. She felt anxious, like she had this urgency pulsing through her body to see Stella, to make sure she was alright.

"Hey, so...what?" Reki put their hand on Zina's, and it pulled her back to herself enough that she looked at them. "Zina, what happened?"

"She's my mate, and I didn't even know Sozarins had mates. Pazin told me last night like it was the most normal thing in the world. Apparently, my face is glittering more than normal, and that's why I've been so fucking itchy. And now this poor human, who is just here on vacation, is the object of my biological obsession. And also, I do actually really like her, but our date was supposed to be fake, so I don't know what to do." Zina stopped, and Reki stared at her, their mouth slightly agape.

"Wow! So...ok. So, you have a mate! That's amazing news, Zina!" Reki said, catching up with everything she'd dumped on them. "You've always wanted to, like, find someone and settle down, right?"

"Yes, but I wanted them to also want that!" Zina said, stopping short as a customer approached the bar.

Reki took one for the team and helped the guest. When they'd left with their drink, Zina turned to them again. "Our date was nice, but it was fake, Reki."

"Well, do you know she would have said no to a real date? Like, did you ask her?"

Zina thought for a moment. "No..."

"Ok, well, maybe let's start with that? I know it's overwhelming, but you said she was nice, so try just talking to her about it?" Reki tilted their head as they spoke, forcing Zina to look at them.

"Well, there's another issue," Zina said softly.

Reki just waited.

"I may have...run away from her at the end of the date," Zina winced. Reki rubbed their temples.

"Why exactly did you do that?" They asked, not unkindly.

"Well, so...Sozarins have these tentacles...inside," Zina whispered, eyebrows raised. Reki nodded. "And they don't ever come out, except one did yesterday when I was with her, and I panicked and...ran."

"I see," Reki said. Zina could tell they were trying not to laugh.

"Stop! It's not funny," Zina whispered, lightly slapping their arm.

"It kind of is, though," Reki said, smiling. Zina frowned at them.

"Ok, ok, so you ran away because you were freaked out about the tentacle thing. I think you should just tell her that, too. I bet she will understand!" Reki patted

Zina's hand. "Don't do the thing, Zina. The thing that always happens in movies and books where you just don't talk to the other person, and you make a whole bunch of drama out of something that could have been a quick chat." Reki said that last part as they headed out to take orders from the groups of guests that had started to appear around the beach.

Just talk to Stella — Zina could do that—just a conversation.

AS IT TURNED OUT, the thought of "just a conversation" completely derailed Zina for the entire first half of the day. She had never spilled a drink since she started this job, and she managed to spill three within the first two hours she was there.

Her breath caught in her chest as she looked up about halfway through her shift to see a few of Stella's friends dropping their bags onto lounge chairs not far from the bar. Stella wasn't with them, though. Zina's heart sank. It was her turn to make rounds, though, so she headed over to them. Maybe they wouldn't remember her.

"Oh, it's you!" one of Stella's friends called out, waving as Zina approached.

"Hey guys," Zina said, trying to sound completely chill and normal.

"We should probably introduce ourselves now that you and Stella…" one of the friends, the one with pink at the ends of her long black hair, said.

"Of course. I'm Zina, I use she/her," Zina said, not wanting to make them say "now that you and Stella fucked" out loud.

"I'm Lenny, she/her," the one with the pink hair said. She gestured to the willowy person with dark brown skin to her right. "This is my girlfriend Dana, also she/her."

"I'm Taylor," a human with golden hair and bright blue eyes chimed in. "They/them."

"Marie!" the last friend chimed in. "She/her," she added with a smile. Her glossy black curls bounced a bit as she spoke.

"Good to meet you all. Is Stella joining you today?" Zina tried not to sound desperate.

"She's doing her own thing today," Dana said. "She likes to have some alone time to recharge."

"I can understand that," Zina said.

"We could…give you her number, though? If you didn't get it already?" Lenny said, eyebrows raised.

Shit, Zina hadn't even thought of that when she'd been on her date with Stella yesterday. Now her friends would think she was an asshole. She couldn't say no, though … she wanted to send Stella a note apologizing for running off.

"I'd love that, thanks," Zina said, and Lenny gave her

a broad smile. Maybe they wouldn't all think she was terrible after all.

Lenny pulled a tiny notepad and pen out of her floral tote bag and quickly scribbled a number on it. "Earth, USA country code," she said, handing Zina the paper.

"Thank you," she said, holding it awkwardly. Nowhere to put it with no pockets … "Can I get you guys anything to drink?"

"Just water for me," Dana said, and the others nodded.

"Water for everyone?" Zina asked, and they all agreed.

As Zina filled cups with ice and water, Reki patted her on the shoulder.

"You're going to ask her to talk?"

"Yes, Reki, I'm going to ask her to talk," Zina said, though the idea made her well and truly a mess. She almost hoped she would just run into Stella rather than send her a message and risk Stella leaving her on read. It was no less than Zina deserved after running away like that.

The rest of the morning passed in a blur. Zina's thoughts wandered to Stella every few moments, but she fought with herself not to let her imagination run too wild. Stars, she didn't need her tentacle coming out again while she was at work.

Around midday, she said goodbye to Reki, who had promised to go with her to the party that night to be her wingperson. In reality, they probably just wanted to watch Zina flounder. Zina knew they had her back, even if they did want to take enjoyment from her awkwardness.

As she walked to the small spa, Zina hoped beyond hope that maybe Stella was there.

She didn't see Stella when she arrived. She thought about the scrap of paper that was now in her tote bag. She should send Stella a message now, and maybe they could talk before the party. She wanted to, but something deep in her was afraid of what Stella might say.

She took a deep breath and decided that she needed to do it anyway. Opening her tote bag, she felt around for the paper. Her hand sensed wetness, and she pulled it back with a disgruntled "eugh". She reached back in to find that her bottle of apple juice was leaking.

Zina groaned and pulled the damp, sticky bottle out, throwing it in the trash. Stars, of course, this would happen to her when she happened to have paper in her bag. She never used paper.

She peered into the bag again and found the sad, soggy slip of paper crumpled at the bottom. The ink had smeared and bled, and there was no way she was going to be able to make out those numbers.

Zina's head began to ache. Why was she like this? Her best hope now was to catch Stella at the party–and figure out how to casually mention that Stella is her mate. That should be super simple, right?

chapter nine

Stella was feeling more centered after a quiet day of reading out on her little porch among the stars. She was ready to dance the night away with her friends. Maybe she would even see Breta again. She could at least *try* to flirt. She owed it to herself to try to have fun. It was her birthday, after all.

This party was not in the main atrium, but instead in a massive ballroom on the other side of the space station. It was hexagonal, with a large, open main floor and a balcony that ran around the entire top perimeter of the room. A menagerie of colorful lights shifted around the space, and the deep pulsing of the bass ran through Stella's body. She didn't go out to the clubs much back on Earth, but she had always loved dancing. She smiled, her anxiety settling as she walked further into the party with her friends by her side.

Weirdly enough, this was one of the only events at the resort that *did* allow clothing. The fact that going out in an outfit was starting to feel novel almost made Stella laugh at herself. She had brought her most obnoxious, incredible silver glittery cocktail dress for this occasion, and she felt pretty as the lights caught its shimmer.

"I'm going to get a drink!" Taylor said, straining to talk over the music. "Anyone want anything?"

Stella hesitated for a moment, worried that perhaps Zina would be at the bar–but no, even if she was, Stella had resolved to be completely chill and normal about it.

"I do!" Stella said, moving to follow Taylor before she could think too hard about it.

They approached the bar, and Stella couldn't stop herself from doing a quick scan—no sign of a swishy purple ponytail. Stella was relieved... or maybe disappointed? She couldn't tell, and she was tired of trying to decipher herself.

"Can I have a sex on the beach, please?" she asked the bartender when they came over to her and Taylor. They nodded and busied themselves with the drinks.

"If it isn't the lovely Stella, shining just as brightly as her namesakes." A vaguely familiar voice sounded behind her, and she turned to find Breta leaning against the bar.

"Oh, Breta, wasn't it? Good to see you again, how are you tonight?" Stella smiled, clearing her mind, giving herself permission to go for this, even if she still really just wanted Zina.

"I'm better now that I know you're here," Breta said with a smile. The bartender returned then, sliding Stella's drink across the counter to her. She gave them a grateful nod and took a big sip, letting the tangy grapefruit wash over her taste buds.

"Any chance you might want to dance with me?" Breta asked.

Stella hesitated for a moment, but then nodded. "Yeah, sure, I'd like to dance." She turned to make sure Taylor knew she was taking off, but Taylor was already shooing her away with a laugh.

Breta offered Stella her hand, which she took. It felt... fine. It didn't send a thrill through her like it had when Zina touched her.

They found a spot on the edge of the mass of dancing people and began to move with the music. Stella let her body take over, her hips swaying to the beat. Breta wasn't a bad dancer, and she smiled at Stella, keeping hold of her hand.

Stella was having fun, trying to let go of the thoughts that had been plaguing her when she caught the flash of shimmery purple out of the corner of her eye. Before she knew what was happening, Zina was there, barely a foot away, looking right at her. Her perfect purple lips were parted as if she was about to speak, but got distracted. Stella just stared back–she was magnificent here under the club lights.

Breta cleared her throat loudly enough to be heard over the music, which startled Stella into action.

"Oh, Breta, do you know Zina?" she said in a rush, trying to make her voice carry.

Breta nodded to Zina with a polite smile. Zina didn't take her eyes off Stella.

"Mind if I cut in?" Zina asked, and Stella's stomach did an anxious flip.

Stella wanted to glance at Breta, certain that she would be annoyed, but she couldn't look away from Zina's perfect face.

"Of course," Breta said finally, releasing Stella's hand and melting away into the crowd. Stella didn't even notice which way she went.

Zina looked amazing–she wore tailored black ankle pants and a buttoned-up cropped vest that matched. It had shimmering magenta embroidery on the vest's lapel and down the side of the pant leg. The vest was ... very low cut, and Stella's eyes were somehow even more drawn to Zina's cleavage in this outfit than they had been when she was naked.

"Stella," Zina said, and the sound of her name on Zina's lips sent a shiver down her spine.

"Zina, I..." Stella began, but hesitated, unsure how to broach such an awkward topic.

"Stella, I'm so sorry I ran off like that yesterday. I got overwhelmed, what you saw in the hot tub..." Zina paused, and Stella could read her genuine anxiety on her face. "Well, that doesn't usually happen."

"I thought you hated me and couldn't stand to be around me, or I offended you terribly or something," Stella said, searching Zina's face.

"Hate you! No," Zina laughed. "No, it's the opposite, actually. I really like you, Stella, and I found myself wishing I could actually fuck you yesterday. I didn't want it to be fake anymore." Zina looked almost frightened as she said this–surely she wasn't worried Stella would reject her?

"Are you being so serious right now?" Stella asked. If Zina were telling the truth, Stella would drag her out of this club and back to her room right now.

"I mean...yes, I'm being serious. Have you seen yourself? You're stunning and also really funny and easy to be around." Zina gestured to Stella as she spoke, her expression earnest.

"And do you...still want to do that?" Stella asked hesitantly.

"Do what?"

"Fuck," Stella said, lowering her voice.

"Oh! Yeah! Yes," Zina answered, nodding. "Yes, I really do. If you do!"

"We're leaving," Stella grabbed Zina's hand, the contact zinging a thrill up her arm. She started making her way through the crowd toward the door. Thankfully, she was able to catch Dana's eye without stopping, and Dana saw Zina being dragged behind her. Dana smiled and nodded at Stella–her friends would know she was safe.

Once they left the party, Stella started to lead Zina toward the main atrium and all the way across the station the way they'd come, but Zina resisted, slowing to a stop.

Stella turned to look at her, worry filling her in a rush. Maybe she had changed her mind already?

But no, Zina was smiling. "Do you want to take the shortcut?"

Stella nodded, following Zina to an unassuming door at the end of the nearest hallway, her pulse pounding in her ears. This was really about to happen.

She barely paid any attention to the labyrinth of slate gray halls that they entered. They were alone for a long while, until Zina suddenly stopped and pulled Stella into an alcove and gently put two fingers against Stella's lips. Stella looked up at her, wide-eyed, about to ask what, exactly, was happening–but then she heard the footsteps, the voices.

Zina winked at her, and Stella tried to fight against the sensation of her knees going weak. God, this alien was so fucking pretty.

When the voices had faded, Zina kept hold of Stella's hand and led her back out into the maze of hallways. Anticipation tingled from Stella's fingers all the way up to her sternum.

They finally emerged in a spot Stella recognized, fairly close to the entrance of her hallway.

"You're going to have to tell me what you like," Stella blurted, the thought occurring to her at the same time it left her mouth. She felt embarrassed for a moment, but she thought better of it–she stood by her need to know that information. She refused to feel silly about good communication.

Zina glanced back at her with a smirk. "Stella, I am fairly certain you could do anything at all, and it would turn me on."

Stella's mouth went dry. "But when I touch you..." Zina's hand tightened slightly on hers.

They stepped up to Stella's door, but she hesitated before unlocking it.

Zina watched her closely. "When you touch me, I want you to explore my body, and I'll tell you if anything feels good or bad, alright?" Her voice was a sultry whisper, and Stella nodded slowly. "Now unlock the door, pretty girl, so I can get you out of that dress."

Stella obeyed, a pulse of awareness between her legs at Zina's words.

The door swung open, and they both stepped inside. Stella was barely breathing.

Zina raised her hand to caress Stella's cheek, her touch so soft but so intimate, and Stella closed her eyes in pleasure. She wanted to live in that feeling. When she opened her eyes, Zina's gaze was heated, her galaxy eyes so focused on Stella's face that she wanted just to get lost in them.

"Can I kiss you, Stella?"

Stella's breath caught, and she whispered, "Yes."

Zina leaned toward her, and Stella's senses were filled with her scent—it was almost like jasmine, but warmer somehow. When Zina's lips pressed into Stella's, the softness of it almost brought tears to Stella's eyes.

She savored the contact, the feel of Zina pulling her

body in close. Her hand drifted up to cup Zina's jaw, and the touch had Zina pressing in, urging Stella's lips to part with her tongue. Stella let her in, and the taste of her had heat flaring to life all over Stella's body.

Their tongues met, and Stella felt her movements growing more desperate. Zina's chest was pressed against hers, and she wanted to feel every inch of Zina's skin. She wanted everything.

Stella pulled back with a gasp. "Off, please take off your clothes."

Zina chucked and moved to obey. "You too," she said simply, her eyes roving over Stella's body.

Stella didn't take her eyes off Zina as she moved to shimmy out of her dress.

Once it was pooled around her feet on the floor, Zina quickly stripped out of her clothes, her strange eyes firmly fixed on Stella's. Stella had never felt tension this thick; it crackled in the air between them like static.

She had seen Zina naked a lot of times, but this felt different somehow—knowing that she was going to be allowed to touch Zina, explore her body, feel her, bring her pleasure ...

Zina's gaze darted to the spot between Stella's thighs that now pulsed with her heartbeat.

"Stella..." Her name on Zina's lips was a plea.

"Zina, I'd like to touch you," Stella whispered.

Before she registered Zina's movement, she was being scooped up into strong purple arms and carried across the room. Zina set her gently down on the bed, and every single place where her hands touched Stella sent chills running across her skin.

Stella wanted to know every way she could make Zina's body sing with pleasure. The thought of it made her squeeze her thighs together, desperately seeking any bit of friction she could get.

"I'll let you touch me, sweet girl, but then I'm going to fuck you. Alright?" Zina's voice was gentle as she moved to lie back on the bed next to Stella.

"You'd better," Stella said with a laugh, rolling to her knees and positioning herself between Zina's legs.

First, she leaned up to kiss Zina again, this time with no barrier blocking the sensation of their bodies pressed together. Stella moaned at the joy of it–god is this what she'd been missing?

She trailed kisses down Zina's neck, drinking in the scent of her. When she got to Zina's chest, she gave one of her nipples a tentative lick. When Zina sucked in a breath, Stella grew bolder, taking her nipple into her mouth and stroking it with her tongue. The sound Zina made would live rent-free in Stella's mind, that was for sure.

As she worked Zina's tit with her mouth, she slid her other hand gently up Zina's thigh. So gently, the tips of her fingers found the slit at the front of Zina's pelvis. When she made contact there, Zina cursed.

"Fuck, Stella, please don't tease me," Zina said, breathless.

Stella released Zina's nipple from her mouth with a

quiet pop and smiled up at her. She held Zina's gaze as she gently ran her fingers along the length of Zina's slit.

"Can I fuck you with my fingers here?" Stella asked.

Zina nodded. "I think I'll die if you don't, actually."

Stella pressed one of her fingers in and gasped—it was impossibly slick and warm just inside the opening, and something moved against her finger, wrapping around it as she worked it in further.

Feeling more confident, Stella withdrew enough to add a second finger, and Zina ground her hips against Stella's hand.

"You're so wet, Zina. Tell me where it feels best for me to touch," Stella said, breathless.

"There's a tiny ridge, a lot like the ones on my face, it's right inside the top of..." Zina trailed off as Stella's fingers made contact with the hard ridge. It was on the outer wall, right at the top. "Fuck," Zina hissed.

Stella smiled and began to rub tiny circles with the pad of her finger on the ridge.

Watching Zina writhe under her touch like this ... Stella felt her own wetness between her thighs. She kept up the motion with her hand and moved to straddle Zina's leg. She had more ridges on her thighs; Stella wondered if ...

As she began to grind her clit on Zina's thigh ridges, Zina cried out, her hands gripping Stella's legs. Stella didn't stop moving, though. She worked herself and Zina at the same time, grinding and rubbing until a sheen of sweat dotted her brow. She had never felt more alive, her own pleasure slowly building in her as she stroked Zina.

Stella had entirely lost track of the time, so lost in every one of Zina's moans and breaths.

Zina sucked in a sharp breath, closing her eyes, her back arching, and whatever was inside her slit wrapped tight around Stella's fingers and began to vibrate. "Stella!" Zina cried, and Stella knew she was coming.

Seeing Zina's pleasure, feeling it, sent a wave of sensation through Stella's whole body. God help her, she wanted to do it again.

"Fuck, Zina, that was the hottest thing I've ever seen," Stella said, panting.

Zina was out of breath too, but she smiled up at Stella. "But we're just getting started, sweet girl. I'll show you more than that." And then, Zina was moving.

Stella was on her back in an instant, Zina's weight pressing into her. The way it felt to have Zina's tits smushed up against hers was going to haunt her for the rest of her life, she thought.

"I'm going to fuck you, Stella, and you're going to tell me if anything hurts, alright?" Zina's purple lashes brushed her glittery cheeks as she glanced down to where her hips sat cradled in Stella's.

"I don't understand, do you have a str ..." Stella trailed off as the tentacle she'd seen in the hot tub the other day slipped out of Zina's slit. "Oh!"

"This part is new for me, too. It uh ... the tentacle normally stays inside," Zina said.

Stella wanted to feel it–she wanted Zina to fill her up. She reached her hand up and stroked her thumb along Zina's cheek ridge, and Zina shuddered.

"Stars," she whispered. "I need to be inside you."

Stella nodded, and Zina pulled her hips back just enough that the tentacle sought out Stella's entrance. Just the tip of it stroked her clit, pulling a gasp from her, before it shifted down, softly brushing her cunt. Zina's face was focused; she looked to be fighting against becoming overwhelmed with whatever she could feel through her tentacle.

"Take a deep breath for me," Zina whispered. Stella filled her lungs with air as Zina pushed herself in. The sensation of it was relief and rightness, and as Stella exhaled, she felt so pleasantly full. Zina groaned, and Stella wanted more.

"Please," Stella begged.

Zina's tentacle pushed further into her, pressing against her inner walls. Zina bent and pressed first one kiss, then another, to Stella's temples. "You're taking it so well, sweet girl. Take whatever you need."

Stella nearly came undone at Zina's words, at the thought that Zina was so tight inside her. She ground her hips, taking Zina even further in, and Zina cried out in pleasure.

Stella couldn't quite see what was happening where they were joined, but it felt like there was pressure on her clit that hadn't been there a moment before. She glanced at Zina's arms, still holding her up on either side of Stella's body. If her hands were there, then what ...

Whatever was touching her began rubbing her, fast, and suddenly she didn't care even a little bit what was happening, she just wanted to come. She rode Zina's tentacle, moving her hands to cup Zina's perfect tits. She pinched, and Zina cried out, "Fuck!"

And then, Stella had the distinct pleasure of feeling Zina's tentacle inside her as she came. A breathy moan escaped Zina's throat, and she bent forward over Stella, her body wracked with pleasure. The sight of it, combined with the full feeling and the unyielding motion against her clit had Stella crying out as well.

Her orgasm started in her toes, tingling all the way up her legs, until the tightness reached her lower back, and then she was coming, and every squeeze of her walls around Zina's now-vibrating tentacle was ecstasy like she'd never known.

Zina covered Stella's body with her own, embracing her, still buried inside her. They both breathed heavily, trying to recover from what had just happened.

Stella wanted to do it a million more times.

chapter ten

Zina glanced down at Stella as she slept, her head resting on Zina's shoulder. She had fallen asleep not long after they crawled back in bed together to snuggle after they'd showered together.

She was perfect.

Sweet and fun and open—Zina was completely obsessed with her human mate.

Being with Stella had been incredible, but she still hadn't told her the truth. She needed to tell Stella about the Sozarins-having-mates situation. The thought of ruining what they'd shared had Zina's heart racing with anxiety. She didn't want to do anything to upset Stella or make her think she had slept with her for the wrong reasons.

Zina *was* drawn to Stella, but it wasn't just physical. She really liked Stella, and she knew without a doubt that feeling could grow into something much more serious with a little time.

Zina sighed. She didn't know what to do. It's not as if she could just wake Stella up right now and tell her. What would she even say? *"Oh yeah, by the way, we're biologically and spiritually predetermined to be together forever."*

She knew enough about humans to know that, usually, no such bond existed for them. Stars, she'd known some species had a mating situation, but she'd never even thought to suspect that Sozarins might.

She was in so over her head.

Zina sat up most of the night, worried. She did force herself to take a bit of time to enjoy Stella's closeness, but her thoughts were a mess.

She glanced at the clock on the nightstand and rolled her eyes. She needed to get ready for her shift soon. Stars, she was going to be exhausted.

Very gently, Zina shifted Stella's head over onto the pillow and slipped out of bed. She gathered her discarded pile of clothes and then bent over Stella, gently kissing her cheek before she turned to go.

Exhaustion hung heavy on her as she walked back to her room. She had no idea how she would ever make it through the day.

She'd taken the shortcut through the back hallways, and they were mostly quiet this early. Zina rounded the final corner on her route and was so out of it that she almost ran straight into a very startled Pazin.

"Zina!" they said, putting their hands out in front of them to steady her.

"Pazin, I'm so sorry!" she said, clutching her clothes close to her.

Pazin's eyes darted to the bundle, and they smiled at her.

"You were at the party last night! Did you successfully court your mate?" They sounded so enthusiastic that Zina couldn't help but smile at them.

"I did, yes. Thanks again for your help the other day, Pazin."

"Oh, of course, I am happy to help in any way I can! It is a great and precious gift when a Sozarin finds their mate. Though, make sure you're careful unless the two of you are trying to create."

The words pinged through Zina's tired mind, but she couldn't make sense of what Pazin had said.

"What do you mean be careful? Create what exactly?" Zina searched Pazin's face, but sadly, the answer was not written there.

"Oh! Well, Sozarin mated pairs are especially fertile. Particularly while your ridges are still glittering," they gestured to Zina's face, and her fingers automatically went to her cheek ridge as if she would be able to feel it glittering.

"Oh, my mate is a human woman, so..." Zina said, shrugging. It had never crossed her mind that she could start a family by accident; she was only attracted to other women.

Pazin studied her for what felt like eternity, their eyebrows furrowed in confusion. "Yes...and?"

This was the most horrifically awkward conversation Zina had ever experienced.

"And...well, I suppose it's not that we're both women, but we both have...you know," Zina said.

"Zina, as a mated Sozarin, you are able to biologically impregnate your mate, no matter their anatomical makeup."

Zina felt like she might be dreaming–that was it. She fell asleep back in the bed with Stella ...

"Your tentacle, when your body has released the mating hormones, is able to disperse whatever genetic material is needed to create new life. So, unless you're wanting to do that with your partner right now..."

"I need to get to the med bay," Zina said, her mind stumbling through the implications of what Pazin was telling her.

"Do you want me to go with you?" Pazin asked, their face again showing their concern.

"No, that's alright, Pazin, I'll handle it, but thank you." Zina nodded and turned to head down the hallway to her left. She fumbled with her clothes as she walked, digging her device out of her pants pocket.

TEXT: I'm going to be in late for sure, but maybe not at all. Have a health thing to deal with.

Zina sent the message off to Reki and picked up her pace to get to the station's medical bay. She needed to get Stella some birth control as soon as possible. She knew it wasn't particularly likely that one night together would result in a pregnancy, but she didn't want to mess around. If she had known she could get Stella pregnant, she would have taken a lot of precautions last night and made sure Stella was consenting to the risks.

Stars, how could she have had no idea? Did she know fucking nothing about her own species?

Frustration pulsed through her as she walked. How could she be so clueless?

The thought that her ignorance could leave Stella to deal with a medical situation ...

She needed to calm down. Get the meds, find Stella, and tell her the truth. That's all she had to do. Simple— and yet, so, so complicated.

chapter eleven

Stella had been vaguely aware of the sensation of a kiss on her cheek as she slept. When she woke up fully, the memory of that made her smile–and then she remembered everything else, and she couldn't contain her grin.

Everything about it had been perfect. She moved to get up from the bed and felt a pleasant ache between her legs. Visions of Zina's face as she'd fucked Stella replayed in her mind. She wanted Zina again, wanted to try everything with her.

The realization that she and her friends only had a few days left of their vacation had sadness and anxiety spiking behind Stella's sternum, rushing in to replace the joy she'd been feeling only a second before.

But no, she couldn't let that ruin her positive feelings. She had known going into it that nothing more could come of being with Zina, and she'd wanted to do it

anyway. That had always been the point; she was here to get laid, not to get a girlfriend.

Did Stella want that? She examined her feelings, trying to decipher what was post-sex cozy feelings and what might remain once the glow had faded. But she would date Zina, she realized. She absolutely would. She was easy to be around and made Stella feel seen and safe, and it was just–fun to be with her.

She forced that thought to the back of her mind with a sigh and decided instead to replay her mental images of Zina coming undone under her touch.

Her friends had decided that room service was in order that morning, so Stella slipped into her pajamas before padding down the hall to knock on Dana and Lenny's door. Dana opened it after a moment and waved her in.

Stella couldn't help but smile at the scene before her– Marie sat up at the head of the bed, snuggled up with Lenny. Taylor sat in the chair that went with the little desk, and they were all looking at the breakfast menu on their phones.

"Ooooh, can we get mimosas?" Marie asked.

"I think I just want coffee, but you guys should go in on a pitcher," Taylor said. "Everything sounds so good right now."

"Seriously, should we just get one of everything?" Lenny asked with a chuckle.

Marie's eyebrows rose into an expression that said *maybe we should.*

"No, we can't! That would be way too much food," Lenny said, elbowing Marie.

"Dana, what are you getting?" Taylor asked, glancing up from their phone and giving Stella a smile.

"You left early last night!" Lenny said, beaming at Stella. "Anything you want to share with the class?"

Stella laughed, "Zina and I hooked up again. It was… really fun." She knew she was probably blushing.

"Are you going to tell us more than you did last time?" Marie asked. "Please! I'm begging. I need to know!"

"Well, apparently Sozarins have tentacles in their slits," Stella said.

"No way! That's so cool," Taylor said, eyes wide.

"Um, yeah, it was … cool," Stella said with a grin.

"She fucked you with it?!" Lenny asked.

Stella nodded, "She absolutely did." She moved to sit down on the foot of the bed, folding her feet under her.

"This Sozarin sunrise thing sounds good, maybe I'll try that," Marie said, and Stella was grateful that the attention had turned away from her again.

Dana sat down next to her and leaned in. "You didn't really sleep with her the other day, did you?"

Stella jerked her head to look at Dana, and her mouth popped open in surprise. She really thought she'd done a good job of arranging the whole thing. Dana waited, her face expectant.

"Uh…well, no," Stella said, cringing.

"Yeah, that's what I thought. But you actually did

last night? So that was really your first time?" Dana had known Stella for too long to have missed the truth like that. Stella sighed and nodded.

Dana patted her knee. "I'm really happy for you, Stella. I hope it was everything you hoped it would be."

"It definitely was, and so much more," Stella whispered back. "Dana, I think I like her."

Stella had decided not to think about that, but as usual, she couldn't keep her mouth shut.

"She seems really cool, Stella. If you like her, just spend some more time with her while you can. See how things shake out."

"Dana, do you want to split the Starlight Sampler?" Lenny asked, and Dana's attention shifted to her girlfriend.

"Sure, baby, that sounds great." Dana gave Stella a wink as she finished speaking.

"So what are we doing today, again?" Marie asked. "I can't believe we only have today and tomorrow left before we go home! I feel like I need a whole other week off work."

"Same, it feels like we just got here," Dana added.

"After we eat, we have a break for a good long while to do whatever, and then this afternoon we're going to yoga." Lenny sounded particularly excited about that, but Stella wasn't really looking forward to it. She had never really been a yoga kind of gal, but she had said she would do it to hang out with her friends. The thought of everyone being naked while they did it was still kind of weird to her.

"And tomorrow is naked crafting?" Dana asked with laughter in her voice.

Taylor burst into laughter, too. "Oh god, I forgot about that."

"This is the weirdest and best vacation. I don't know how we'll ever top this with another friend trip." Marie said through her giggles.

"I mean, we could always come back," Stella said, shrugging.

"I'm down." Lenny didn't hesitate. "This place has amazing food and tons of cool stuff to do, and like..." she gestured toward the glass door out to the balcony and the expanse of space beyond. "It's cool as fuck."

"Agreed, this was a great find, Lenny. It's like an old school Sandals resort but like ... better." Taylor nodded as they spoke.

"Yeah, we haven't talked about it much, but the like 80's vaporwave vibes here are really doing it for me," Dana added.

Stella realized that she wanted to come back because of Zina–maybe she would still be there. She remembered what Zina had told her on their date, though. She wanted to move somewhere exciting. The thought of that–of never seeing Zina again–made Stella's throat tighten.

She tried to shake it off. It was ridiculous to have feel-ings for someone so quickly, right? She was just doing the thing that people did: falling for the first person they've slept with. She tried not to feel like a loser for it, but there was no way Zina was feeling the same.

A little part of her mind reminded her, though, that she'd thought the same thing about Zina not wanting to fuck her, and she very obviously *had* wanted to do that …

"Stella," Lenny said her name like it wasn't the first time, and Stella snapped back into the present.

"Sorry!" Stella blurted.

"She's probably daydreaming about her alien girl-friend," Marie said with a friendly smile.

"I was, actually," Stella said with a laugh. "What did you say?"

"I was asking if you think you'll be ready to get into dating when we get back to Earth?" Lenny cocked her head as she spoke.

"Oh!" Stella said, startled by the question. She'd always had some excuse: she was too busy, or too tired, or she thought partners would be weird about her not having had sex before. She thought of Zina–of all the dates she wished she could go on with her. "Maybe," she finally said, not believing she really would even for a minute.

A knock sounded on the door, and Taylor hopped up. "I got it."

Stella assumed it would be the room service, but to her shock, she looked up to find Zina following Taylor back into the room.

Taylor was giving her a look, but Stella ignored it and

focused on Zina. She looked concerned and held a small, white bag in her hand.

"Hey guys," Zina said, giving a polite smile and awkward wave to the room full of Stella's friends.

"Is everything alright?" Stella asked hesitantly, eyeing the bag in Zina's hand.

"Oh, yeah, can I just talk to you for a minute?" Zina asked, gesturing over her shoulder with her thumb.

"Sure, of course!" Stella said, already moving to get up and follow Zina. "I'll be back in a few, guys," she said over her shoulder. Her friends all looked like they would start to squeal with delight when she left the room.

Zina followed her wordlessly back to Stella's room and stayed quiet once the door was shut. Stella stood by the bed, but Zina kept her distance. What on earth was going on? Zina couldn't be breaking up with her ... they weren't even together!

"So ..." Stella said, unable to handle the anticipation.

"I, uh ... brought you this," Zina said, extending the bag she still held toward Stella.

Stella took it, her confusion now nearing a tipping point. She peered inside at what appeared to be a small box–it looked like the sort of box medicine usually came in.

"It's birth control. The, uh...the kind you take after." Zina looked like she wanted to disappear into the floor.

Stella frowned, unsure how exactly to word the question she needed to ask.

"I would have obviously taken more precautions and

everything and made sure you consented, but I just learned about it this morning. I didn't grow up with any other Sozarins around to teach me anything, and I just had no idea that this could happen. It's not an excuse, it's just...that's why. And I'm really sorry, Stella, I didn't mean to do anything risky or against your wishes. So," Zina paused. She looked miserable.

Stella's brain struggled to keep up with what Zina was implying.

"I'm so sorry, can we rewind for a minute?"

Zina nodded.

"So you're telling me that I could get pregnant from what we did last night?"

Zina nodded again.

"And you didn't know that was possible...but you've had sex before, right?"

"So it, uh ... it wasn't a possibility in the past, but it is now, I guess. I talked to my Sozarin friend Pazin about it, and they told me it doesn't matter what sort of anatomy either of us has."

"What do you mean by 'it is now, I guess'?" Stella asked, furrowing her brows, trying to glean any additional meaning from Zina's face. She looked nervous. "I don't understand how you didn't know."

Zina opened her mouth as if to answer, but then closed it, looking away from Stella for a long moment. She closed her eyes and sighed. "Sozarins have mates. Like biological, spiritual perfect matches. The tentacle thing ... that only happens when we find our mate, apparently.

And apparently that tentacle secretes genetic material that is ... fertile." Zina put her hand over her face when she finished speaking.

"I'm so sorry, Stella. I didn't mean for any of this to happen, and I feel horrible for putting your health at risk. You didn't ask for this, and I..."

"Woah, woah, woah," Stella interrupted. "Did you say..."

"You're my mate, Stella."

"Oh, *shit*!" Stella blurted.

Zina's eyes widened in surprise. "I know, I'm sorry, I should have told you as soon as I knew, I just didn't think it would matter because you're just here for a few days."

"That's so hot, holy shit," Stella said, the full meaning of Zina's words sinking in. This was something that happened in the monster romance books she read, not in real life.

"What?" Zina looked even more confused now than she had a moment ago.

"You're telling me that I'm *your* mate–you, the hottest, nicest girl I've ever met?"

Stella knew maybe she should be more annoyed with Zina, but she'd said the other day that she hadn't grown up with Sozarins. How was she supposed to know that her body worked this way? She obviously understood that it wasn't great that they'd had fully unprotected sex without knowing all the risks, and she was here with the birth control ... They could talk about it more later. Right now, Stella wanted to fuck her mate.

"Yes..." Zina said hesitantly. "Stella, I can feel a pull toward you. I have this like drive to protect you and be near you, and obviously I'm super attracted to you, but I also just...really like you." She paused, but Stella could tell there was more she wanted to say. "I know this is a lot..." she began, and Stella knew she was about to apologize again.

"Can we make out?" Stella asked, suddenly, and Zina's brows furrowed even more.

"You...want to do that right now? After what I just told you?"

"Do you *not* want to do that right now?" Stella asked, incredulous.

"Stella, I've wanted to do that every second since I first saw you." Zina's words sent a zip of pleasure straight down Stella's spine.

"So why are you still over there?" Stella asked with a laugh.

With that, Zina finally moved, closing the distance between them. Stella reveled in the feeling of Zina's hands slipping around her waist, tangling in her shirt. Their lips came crashing together in a desperate press, and Stella moaned into Zina's mouth.

Zina gently moved them toward the bed, never letting up the urgency of her kisses. Stella felt the bed against the back of her knees, and she slid back onto it, Zina climbing over her.

Stella's whole world became only the feeling of her body pressed close to Zina's. The softness and heat felt right in every way. She wrapped her arms around Zina's waist and let her fingers roam across the smooth skin of Zina's back. God, she was perfect.

Zina kissed Stella's jaw, her breath tickling her ear. Stella threw her head back in pleasure, overwhelmed at how badly she wanted Zina.

"I want you inside me again," Stella begged in a rushed whisper, and Zina chuckled softly.

"You'll have me, perfect girl, but not the way you think," Zina said softly into Stella's ear, her hand punctuating her words by slipping between Stella's legs.

Zina began to work her, gently, just the tips of her fingers grazing all of Stella's sensitive places until she longed to shift her hips and slip Zina's fingers inside her.

Zina stayed her course, though, patiently touching, softly working Stella's body into feeling its pleasure. It was the most sensual thing Stella had ever experienced.

After an impossibly long time, Zina slipped in first, one finger … then two. Stella worked her hips into the feeling, wanting more. Zina watched her, rapt at every sound and movement. Her galaxy eyes were almost black, her pupils blown wide with interest.

"Take a deep breath, and tell me if anything is too much," Zina said, holding Stella's gaze. Stella nodded.

It must have been three fingers as Zina pushed back in; the sensation was stronger, but not at all uncomfortable. Zina slowly worked her, thrusting her fingers in and out, and Stella would have blushed at the wet sounds she heard if Zina did not seem so completely enthralled with watching what she was doing.

Then, Zina began to stroke Stella's clit along with the steady in and out motion she was making, and Stella was so keyed up that she immediately felt her orgasm building. Within moments, it was rushing over her, a great wave of pleasure that lit up every nerve in her body. She wasn't even sure if she made a sound, but she could feel herself clamping down on Zina's fingers.

Zina moaned, "Fuck," which in turn made Stella clamp down with another aftershock.

They looked at each other for a long moment after, before Zina spoke.

"I think you're ready now."

Stella felt incredible, but she knew another orgasm was just under the surface for her. She quirked a brow at Zina in question.

"Just relax your muscles for me, pretty girl. I know you can take it," Zina said, grabbing the small bottle of lube from Stella's nightstand and spreading it over her hand and wrist.

Stella watched, rapt, as Zina squeezed the tips of her fingers together. She felt them press against her entrance, slipping in just a bit before meeting resistance.

"Breathe," Zina said, pressing so slowly further in.

Stella obeyed, pulling air deep into her lungs, pressing down to relax and coax her body to make room for Zina.

"Good," Zina whispered, slipping further in. The

sensation of fullness bordered on pain, but Stella had the urge to grind her hips and take more. She wanted to be *full*.

"You're doing so well, Stella; just a bit more and I'll be inside you up to my wrist." Zina looked like she was having a religious experience. Stella wished she could see the place where their bodies joined.

Stella kept breathing, kept relaxing, until the resistance lessened, and the feeling of fullness peaked. "Shit," Stella squeaked, breathless. "Zina, touch me, please."

Zina didn't hesitate. She brought her free hand up to Stella's clit and began to rub, quick, light strokes.

That sensation, combined with the intensity of Zina's entire hand inside her, was too much for Stella. A sheen of sweat formed on her brow, and her pleasure overwhelmed her. She felt like she left reality and entered another plane of existence.

"Fuck, Stella, you're so tight on my hand," Zina said, and Stella glanced down to see that her tentacles were protruding.

The sight of it was so erotic that Stella couldn't hold back her orgasm any longer. She came harder than she ever had before. Her toes were numb, and the pleasure radiated down the backs of her thighs. The sensation of release was hot and bright.

"Oh fuck," Zina said, "you just squirted all over my hand."

Stella thought she might die from pleasure. Despite the intensity of what she felt, she reached her hand toward Zina's tentacles and let her fingers tangle in them gently. Zina swore again and cried out, bending over Stella. Her tentacles suddenly became slick to the touch, and Stella slowly pulled her hand away to find it glistening with a shimmery purple slime.

Zina looked up at Stella, breathless, and began to very slowly and carefully pull her hand out of Stella. When she finally slid out, Stella felt empty and sated.

"That," Zina began, gesturing to Stella's hand that still shimmered with slime, "is why you need to take that birth control I brought."

Stella couldn't help the laugh that bubbled out of her. Who would have thought her lesbian alien mate could get her pregnant with pretty glittery slime.

"Alright, I'll take it," Stella said as she finished her bout of laughter. Zina was smiling, too.

A knock sounded at the door, and they both looked at each other in panic.

"Shit! Yoga!" Stella said.

"Hey are you still coming to yoga class or..." Lenny's voice sounded outside the door.

"Uh...No! Sorry!" Stella called and grimaced.

"Didn't think so," Lenny said. She sounded smug, not angry, though.

"So...can I make you come again?" Stella asked. Zina laughed and pulled Stella in close to her, nuzzling her face into Stella's neck.

"Yes, pretty girl, but only after I snuggle you for a minute."

chapter twelve

Zina thought absently that this was how she wanted to spend every night of her life–limp and pleasantly exhausted with her mate draped across her. Stella's body pressed against hers felt like Zina had finally come home.

Stella nestled her face into Zina's neck, and the surge of emotions that Zina experienced nearly took her breath away. She was getting well and truly attached to this pretty human.

"What are we going to do about all this, then?" Stella said, her voice barely above a whisper.

Zina knew what she *wanted* to do. What they should do, however, was very different. When Zina didn't answer right away, Stella pulled back to study her face.

"I want you to come to Earth with me," Stella said. Zina felt her mouth pop open in shock.

"You can't mean that, we just met a few days ago ..."

Zina began to recite the long list of reasons that filled her mind of why they shouldn't just be together, even though that's what she wanted more than she'd ever wanted anything in her life. She just wanted to be sure that's what would make Stella happy, too. She would rather suffer through being apart than be together knowing that she was ruining Stella's life.

"I do mean it. I want to be with you, Zina." Stella cupped Zina's face in her perfect hand, and the look on her face made Zina believe she meant what she said.

"I need you to take some time to think about it, please. I don't want to barge into your life and take over. I want to be with you, Stella, more than anything. It will just make me feel better if you think about it for a while to be sure." Speaking the words made Zina's heart nearly break in two.

Stella searched her face for a long moment, and Zina could see tears gathering in her eyes. She wanted to throw herself out into the vacuum of space for having caused those tears to appear.

"Tomorrow is our last day ..." Stella said, trailing off.

"I know," Zina whispered.

"You want me to...go back to Earth and think about it for a while." A tear fell from Stella's eye, racing down her cheek, and Zina reached up to brush it away. She pulled Stella in close, cradling her head against her chest.

"I think that's what's best, for both of us. You, so that you have time to make sure you really want a live-in alien girlfriend, and me so that I can be sure that I won't be ruining your life if I come to Earth with you."

Stella nodded against Zina's chest, and her own throat tightened to the point of pain.

"I just...need you to be sure. I can feel myself falling in love with you with every passing second," Zina whispered, her voice hoarse.

"I'll take some time like you've asked, but I don't think it will make me want you any less," Stella said, still buried against Zina's chest. Zina only ran her hand gently through Stella's hair, holding her.

After what could have been a few minutes or a few hours, Stella stirred.

"I'm starving," she said. A loud grumble of her stomach punctuated her statement.

Zina immediately felt terrible that she hadn't thought to get them food sooner. Stella gave her a bit of room to roll over and grab her content device from her tote bag on the floor.

"What sounds good? I can get us anything you want," Zina said.

"Oh, I thought there was only the one spot that did room service?" Stella asked.

"Officially, yes, but I know a few people," Zina said with a smile.

"Honestly? I really want like ... a pizza and breadsticks. Is that a thing here?"

Zina chuckled, "Baby, this place is like an Earth-

1980's wet dream. Of course, there's pizza. What toppings are your favorite?"

Stella laughed a bit as she answered, "I'm good with whatever you want."

"No, no, sweet girl, that isn't what I asked." Zina rolled back over and kissed her cheek.

"My favorite is kind of weird..."

"I don't care, tell me," Zina said, stroking her finger down Stella's cheek.

"I like barbeque sauce, green peppers, onions, black olives, and pepperoni," Stella said, a hilariously guilty look on her face.

"Oh, so not really that weird at all," Zina said with a shrug. "You said you wanted breadsticks, too? There are a bunch of sauces that can come with it. What sounds good?" Zina handed Stella her device and took the opportunity to admire Stella's perfect face as she studied the menu.

Once she had picked her sauce, Zina placed the order.

"What should we do until the food gets here?" Stella asked, a coy expression on her face that made Zina's heart melt.

"Oh, I don't know...I guess I could think of a few things."

"Like what?" Stella asked. "We'd have to be quick, wouldn't we?"

"Let's see..." Zina cupped Stella's breast. She glanced over at the end table where she had noticed the lube earlier. "That's your sex device?" She pointed to the slender purple handle with a tiny cup on one end.

Stella blushed a bit, but nodded.

"Can I use it on you?" Zina asked, hoping desperately that Stella would say yes.

Stella nodded, a small smile curving her perfect lips.

"Good," Zina said, and she moved into a sitting position with her back against the headboard and spread her legs. She patted the space there, wanting Stella to come sit.

"Put your back against me, baby, and just lean your head on my shoulder."

Stella did as Zina asked, and Zina felt her arousal run through her as Stella settled into place, cradled between Zina's legs.

"Good, now spread your legs for me, pretty girl," Zina whispered in Stella's ear.

Once Stella had opened herself, Zina turned on the device, and it began to hum with vibration. First, she slid her fingers through Stella's wetness, letting out a breath at the feeling of it. Stars, she was so soft.

Then she placed the device onto Stella's clit, gently, and began to rub her fingertips around Stella's opening. She just barely pushed her fingers in, moving around in languid motions as she let the device do its work.

Stella was panting in a matter of moments. The gentle hum of the device was hypnotic, and Zina lost herself in the moment. She would never forget this view, looking down over Stella's shoulder to see her perfect body totally at her mercy.

Stella's beautiful tits rose and fell with her heavy breathing, and Zina did not let up. Stella's legs twitched every few seconds, so Zina knew she was close. She very gently wiggled the device against Stella's clit and ... there.

Stella moaned, arching her back as she came for the third time that afternoon. Stella's lower back pressed against Zina's slit, and she could almost *feel* Stella's pleasure in her own body.

Stars, she was so completely and utterly obsessed with this woman.

ZINA COULDN'T AFFORD to miss two days of work in a row, so when it was time, she once again slipped out of Stella's bed. Stella looked so peaceful sleeping there, and it nearly killed Zina to pick up her bag and walk out the door. She promised herself that she would give Stella space to think; she would do what she could to avoid Stella and her friends for the day.

As she walked back to her room, Zina thought about how she would make sure to send Stella a message so they would be able to contact each other once she was home. Then she would leave the ball in Stella's court to decide what she really wanted.

Zina wasn't sure how hard it usually was for a Sozarin to be away from their mate, but she didn't really want to know. Knowing her luck so far, she would just find out that she was going to wither up and die.

She kind of already felt like she might.

Stella was such a light, and Zina wanted to please her, make her happy, be by her side. She realized it was a bit funny how she'd been raised with a Moratari family—Moratari's traditional religion was, essentially, the worship of the stars. And now, Zina had found her very own star to worship.

She imagined what it would be like if Stella really wanted to be with her. It was a life she never dreamed could be within her grasp. They would have a home full of things they both loved. They would live their lives but always come back home to each other. They would share meals, meet each other's families ... maybe even have their own.

Zina hardly noticed when she arrived back in her own room; she was completely lost in her own thoughts. She looked around at the space as she re-did her high ponytail, mentally going through the motions of packing up her things. She hadn't been here all that long, so she didn't have a ton of stuff with her. Most of her things were back at her family's house; she'd moved her things there to store when she gave up her apartment to take this job.

Zina sighed, an overwhelming cocktail of emotions sitting in her chest. Joy and excitement on the one hand—

Stella was glad to be her mate, and that was more than she ever could have hoped for. Sadness and worry, on the other hand, she didn't want to be apart from Stella, even though she knew it was best. And what if Stella decided she didn't want to see Zina again at all?

She tried to force the thought from her mind as she finished her quick preparations for work and headed back out the door.

Of course, today was one of the days Reki had been assigned to work with her by the pool. She knew they would give her an impossibly hard time about everything that had happened–in a loving way, but still.

"Well, look who's back," Reki said as Zina hung her bag behind the bar. She rolled her eyes at them.

"So ... she's a mated gal now, huh?"

"How did you ... Pazin." Zina sighed.

"Yeah, they gave me the scoop. I believe congratulations are in order?" Reki smiled broadly at her. They moved to put away a glass they'd been drying, their serpentine body graceful as they lifted their arm to put it back on a high shelf.

"Well, I don't know if anything will really come of it," Zina said, avoiding Reki's gaze.

Reki froze, and Zina could see out of the corner of her eye that their brows were furrowed.

"What do you mean by that?" Reki asked slowly.

"I mean that my mate is a human who was just here on vacation looking for a good time, and I don't particularly want to ruin her whole life just because I was predetermined to be with her."

"So you're what? Not going to go back to Earth with her? Or take her back home?" Reki sounded more shocked than Zina would have expected.

"No, I told her to take some time and think about it."

"Zina," Reki said, waiting for her to turn and look at them. "Are you serious? You found your *mate*. The one being in the galaxy that you're meant to be with, and you're not going to stay by her side? You're going to just watch her leave?"

The way Reki was saying it gave Zina pause, but she knew she was being reasonable for Stella's sake.

"Reki, obviously, if I were the only one involved here, I wouldn't hesitate, but I'm not. She's a whole person with a whole life, and she doesn't need me just inviting myself to barge in and shake it all up."

"Did you invite yourself? Or did she want you to go?" Reki asked incredulously.

"She..." Zina shook her head and sighed. "She wanted me to go, but Reki, she's never been with anyone before, really. What if she just likes me because she doesn't know what she's missing?"

"Ah, there it is. You're afraid." Reki said, nodding.

"I am not afraid!" Zina's indignance came across stronger than she'd intended ... maybe Reki was on to something.

"You are. You're afraid she will change her mind, and

you're afraid she only wants you because you're mates and not because you're *you*."

With that, Reki moved away to check on the guests who were starting to claim spots around the pool.

Zina leaned against the counter and put her head in her hands. The day had just started, and already she wanted it to be over. Just one day of giving Stella space before she went home couldn't possibly be that bad, right?

chapter thirteen

This was so bad. Bad and terrible and Stella hated it.

Knowing Zina was here, and that she only had one day left before she went home, was ... anxiety-inducing to say the least.

There was good, too, though. She had a *mate* of all things. She'd come on this trip hoping to just fuck someone for the first time, and she'd ended up with Zina.

The last few days had been a lot, but Stella felt excited and optimistic alongside her anxiety.

She headed out the door, finding her friends already congregated in the hallway. It was time for their crafting class, which Marie had requested, if she remembered correctly. Stella wasn't sure what they were even going to make, but the whole concept of a nude crafting class was hilarious to her.

"Who's ready to make some stuff?!" Marie asked excitedly.

The group stopped to grab snacks and fancy coffees before arriving at the craft room. Stella got something called a "galactic latte," and it was purple—the exact same shade as Zina's hair. Stella sighed.

Once they were all settled in the craft room, they listened to their class lead, a massive Trozul named Bok, explain that they would be making tiny models of the space station to take home as souvenirs. The kits that were set out in front of them looked quite intimidating, but Stella was a sucker for mini anything.

Once Bok had explained the project, they each set to work. What was crafting without chatting, though? Stella knew talking with her friends about what was happening with Zina would help her feel better. Her therapist had told her a long time ago that she was a "verbal processor", which Stella took mostly as meaning she needed to yap about things to feel better about them.

"Ok, so story time!" Stella said, and her friends all glanced up at her, eager to hear what she had to say.

"I, uh...Well, Zina is my mate!"

Her friends stared at her in stunned silence for a long moment before Marie cut in. "Wait, do you mean like *MATE* mate? Like in one of those books we read all the time? But REAL?"

Stella nodded. "Yes, that is what I mean. Apparently, Sozarins have them! And Zina didn't know. She does now! But she didn't."

"So what are you like getting married?" Taylor asked.

"No, no! Well, not yet. Well! Ok, so here's the part

that I need to explain and talk with you guys about." Stella felt overwhelmed trying to explain this.

"So I really like Zina, and she really likes me too, and she told me the other day when we were on our fake date that she really wants to move off-world someday, so when she told me that I'm her mate and everything, I was like, 'Oh, you should come to Earth, and we can be together!'" Stella couldn't stop now that she'd started.

"So anyway, she said that she would really like that, but that she's worried maybe I need time to think about it since she's the first person I've really been with. I think she's trying to be respectful and also make sure that I'm not going to change my mind on her, but like, I feel pretty sure about it. She's so smart and funny and kind, and she makes me feel really safe when we're together. So I feel, like, super excited that I have a mate and that it's her, but also I feel sad because she said we should stay away from each other until we leave, and also that I should take some time once I'm back home to think about everything." Stella was out of breath.

"Wait, did you say fake date?" Lenny asked.

"Ooooh...yes, I did." Stella chuckled nervously. "Well, that's part of why I think she's so nice! I told her when I was at the bar the other day that I felt stressed about trying to hook up with someone, so she offered to pretend to do it just so that I could like ... do my own thing without you guys worrying about it so much." Stella felt worse and worse about what she'd done as she spoke.

"Girl, you could have just asked us to back off!" Dana said with a laugh.

"Seriously, you're wild for doing all of that," Lenny added.

"I'm really sorry, I just...it meant a lot to me that you guys organized this trip so I could have a shot at that, and it is fun to like talk about stuff and scheme with you guys, I just felt overwhelmed, and then Zina offered..."

"No, that's fair, you're just silly," Marie said. "Can we get back to the part where Zina said you should take time to think about stuff?"

"Yeah, it seems like she hasn't heard about the lesbian U-Hauling stereotype we have on Earth," Dana said wryly.

"I certainly would not be beating the allegations. I really want to give it a shot. Like, obviously, I know that if either of us felt like it wasn't working out down the road, something might happen, but ... it just seems like we need to give it a go. And I know we could still give it a go after I go home and take some time to think about it, but I don't want to be away from her." Stella tried to place a tiny palm tree with her tweezers as she spoke, but it just got stuck to the wrong wall of her tiny model.

"I can respect where she's coming from, wanting to like be cautious and sure and not rush," Taylor began, "but we only have one life to live. If you both want it, I think you guys should go for it."

"Yeah, I think so too!" Marie said with a nod.

"So you two aren't seeing each other again at all

before we leave tomorrow? Not even at the club tonight?" Lenny asked.

"Nope, I guess not," Stella said, fighting with her little tube of superglue. Tiny stings of it got everywhere as she tried to dab it onto a mini pool float. She leaned forward, trying to get a good angle to place the tube.

"That's kind of a bummer. I see why you're kind of feeling happy and sad all at once," Lenny said.

Stella pulled back to look up at Lenny and agree with what she'd said, but a sharp pain pulled on her. She looked down and gasped. "Oh shit!"

"What's wrong?" Dana asked, immediately preparing to help Stella.

"I superglued my boob to the edge of the table!" She looked down, and sure enough, the skin of her boob was stuck to the table, pulling painfully whenever she moved slightly.

Lenny started laughing uncontrollably, and Marie was close behind. Stella couldn't help but join them, and soon they were all laughing so hard they were crying.

"This is the most fucking crazy thing we've ever done, fucking naked crafting," Stella said through her gasping laughter.

Bok, the instructor, was smiling, too, when he brought over a tiny bottle of some kind of glue remover they kept on hand. Stella realized she must not be the first person who had glued their naked body to the craft table. She shook her head at herself, laughter finally dying down. Her stomach hurt from it, and she wished Zina had been there to laugh with them, too.

The remainder of diorama crafting was pleasant if uneventful. When they were done, they took a walk around the resort to find some lunch, and they happened to pass by a tiny tattoo shop. Flash designs were hung on the window, and they all stopped to look, pointing out which ones they liked the best.

"Oh, that one is so pretty!" Lenny said, her finger pointing at a leaf that was drawn to look like it was a neon sign.

"Oh yeah, I love that! It's like that one type of plant that's all over the place here, around the pool. I don't know what they're called." Dana said, looking where Lenny had pointed.

"Should we..." Marie said, eyebrows raised.

"I'm down," Taylor answered with a shrug.

"Hell yeah," Dana added, and Lenny nodded enthusiastically next to her.

"Yeah, why not?" Stella said, smiling.

And so they all headed into the tattoo shop and got their cute little leaves. Dana, Stella, and Marie opted for the black-ink version, but Taylor and Lenny chose neon colors that looked incredible.

Whatever technology they had to do the tattoos was super cool and quick; it was almost like a stamp. Each one only took about five minutes total. They were all tattooed and on their way in half an hour.

With time to kill before they went out dancing for

their last night, they decided to do some more window shopping. Several stores carried items from other planets in the system that were hard to find on Earth, which made it really interesting to Stella.

They wandered into a jewelry shop that Lenny had noticed, which had all sorts of pretty things. There were a lot of bold, brightly-colored gems set into pretty shimmering metals that didn't quite look like anything they had on Earth. Stella wandered the displays, not expecting to find anything in particular. She didn't wear much jewelry.

The back corner of the shop had a small display of much daintier jewelry, and Stella perused it until her gaze snagged on a necklace. It was silver or it looked like silver anyway–and the chain was so delicate. It shimmered when it caught the light. There was a charm on the necklace, a little chip of magenta. It was the same shade that Stella had noticed swirled into the galaxy of Zina's irises. Stella reached out and let the charm rest on her fingers. It was teardrop-shaped, and was smaller than the tip of her finger.

She looked up to study the sign on the display and saw a short biography written under the name Helen Lee–she was a jewelry artist from Earth.

Stella took the necklace off its hook without thinking about it more–it was from her home, and it reminded her so much of Zina. She wanted to give it to Zina as a gift, to remember their time together.

She took it to the counter and bought it, giving the

shop attendant a polite smile. They wrapped it for her in a dainty blue box with a ribbon. Stella tucked it into her tote bag, feeling excited at the thought of giving Zina such a gift.

It hadn't occurred to her, though, that she had no way of contacting Zina. Her heart sank.

She was going to have to get creative.

chapter fourteen

Zina had picked up an extra shift that night. She wanted to keep her mind off things and stay as busy as she could until she knew Stella was far away, back home. She and Reki were working the bar at the dance hall for the evening, but it was still fairly early.

Zina had been at war with her own mind all day, trying to convince herself that she was doing the right thing by insisting on keeping her distance. She was exhausted.

Reki had been giving her skeptical looks all afternoon, and they weren't letting up now. Every time they caught Zina moping, they reminded her that her sadness was of her own making.

"Oh look," Reki said, and Zina braced herself for another sassy comment. She was eternally grateful for how honest Reki was with her, even when it was hard, but she was about to tell them to back off. She opened her mouth to snap at them, but froze.

Stella and her friends were just coming through the doors of the dance hall across from the bar. Zina's mouth snapped shut.

"Are you seriously not even going to go talk to her?" Reki asked, this time sounding more gentle and sad than anything else.

Zina's throat felt tight.

"I need to get out of here. Can you cover for me?" Zina asked, and she knew she probably looked pathetic. Reki just nodded, slithering over to her and pulling her into a tight hug.

"Try to actually get some sleep tonight. You'll feel better tomorrow." Reki patted her shoulder, and Zina quickly scooped up her bag and made her exit out the back door.

She collapsed onto her bed and curled up into a ball once she was back in her room. She thought about ordering some dinner delivery, but she wasn't really hungry. Stars, she really was being pathetic.

Refusing to let herself completely wallow in this problem that she had created for herself, she pulled up a show about Earth's flora and fauna, as they called their lifeforms. She'd watched it before, but the soothing voice of the narrator kept bringing her back to it. It was an old show, but apparently, this David guy was important to Earth's culture because of his work with animals. Zina liked the episode with the swimming sloth the best, so that's the one she put on while she heated some food.

Her dinner procured, she curled up on her bed, ready to get lost in her show, when her device pinged.

She looked down and saw a message from an unknown number.

> Sorry, I missed you tonight at the dance hall

Zina looked at the message for a long moment before typing her response.

> I wasn't feeling great, left early

She didn't have to wait long for a reply.

> That's what your friend Reki said.
> They're really nice.

> Ah, so that's how you got my number.

Zina was almost certain she was talking to Stella–it sent a wave of anticipation through her.

> Mhm. I figured just texting wouldn't really count as being together? So maybe this would be ok?

Zina smiled down at her device. Stella's determination was charming and extremely attractive to Zina. She wasn't allowing herself the pleasure of being near her mate–she wouldn't deny herself the chance to just talk with her.

> I think this will be alright

That's good to hear. I missed you
all day

Zina waited before responding–she could see that Stella was typing another message.

I've been thinking about the way you
felt inside me

Zina's mouth went dry.

> Have you?

Mhm, it's hard not to think about

> I've been thinking about you too

What about me?

Zina closed her eyes, and a rush of memories filled the space behind her eyelids. Stars, she'd been thinking about every tiny detail she knew of Stella–her expressive eyebrows, the way she blurted out her thoughts, the feeling of her cunt squeezing her hand ...

> Everything. All of it. Every second
> we've spent together since we met. It
> plays through my mind constantly,
> Stella.

Zina?

Yes, Stella?

I want you to lie back on your bed.

Zina suspected she knew where this was going–she wanted Stella so badly, wanted to make her happy–so she did as Stella asked.

I am

Good. Now spread your legs for me

Alright

Now, tell me about how it felt when your tentacles pulled me so close to you that our cunts were pressed together.

Shit, Zina thought, her arousal hitting her in a wave.

You felt so nice against me, sweet girl. Like we were meant to be connected that way

We are meant to be connected that way, Zina

You were so tight, and I could feel your softness against my opening

It felt so, so good for me too. Do you
remember how wet I was for you?

Stars, yes, I do. You're perfect

I want you to touch yourself for me
now, Zina. I can't be there to make
you feel good, but I can still help.

Zina obeyed her mate, slipping her hand down her
body toward her slit. She felt the tip of one of her tentacles poking out and gasped at how sensitive it was.

Tell me what to do, pretty girl.

I want you to touch yourself gently at
first, imagining it's my fingertips on
you, then my mouth

Zina closed her eyes, running her fingers along the
edge of her slit, images of Stella's pretty curls spilling
across her thigh running through her mind. She imagined the feeling of Stella's soft, warm tongue on her.

I want to feel you more than anything

I'd slowly push my tongue into your
slit, Zina, and I'd let your tentacles
wrap around me

As she read that, her tentacles responded, pushing
out of her; she wanted to feel Stella's warmth.

> You're going to be the death of me, Stella

> No, Zina, I'm going to make you feel alive

Zina continued to work herself with her fingers, her mind playing images and sensations from her time with Stella. All of it, every moment, contributed to Zina's arousal.

> You want me to come for you?

> Yes, Zina. I want that. I wish I was there to see it, to hear the sounds you make

Zina pressed down on her most sensitive spot, rubbing it hard and fast until she came, her tentacles dripping and her body spent.

> I just finished imagining you were touching me, perfect girl

> Good. Sleep well, Zina <3

> Wait! Don't I get to help you get off, too?

> Not this time ... You'll have to do it in person

Zina sighed and stared up at her ceiling, feeling more than a little overwhelmed. What was she going to do?

chapter fifteen

Sexting Zina last night had been one of the most fun things Stella had done in a long time. She was disappointed that she hadn't been able to actually fuck Zina, but ... that had turned out to be a nice alternative.

She stepped out onto her little space bubble balcony for the last time and looked out at the stars. Zina would be looking at these same stars, even when Stella was back down on Earth. It was a nice thought, but something about leaving Zina still wasn't sitting right with Stella.

She respected what Zina wanted and understood why she was worried; she really did. She couldn't leave without saying goodbye, though.

Will you meet me in the lobby garden?

She held her breath and waited for a reply. It was silly–she knew Zina was likely at work.

Just as she was about to stuff her phone into her bag, a message notification popped up.

Now?

Stella hurriedly typed her response.

30 minutes

She was suddenly very grateful the space station had adopted Earth's measures of time to make things comfortable for its human guests.

Of course

Stella took a deep breath and tucked her phone away. Thankfully, she was wearing clothes again when she took the shuttle home. She rummaged around in her tote bag for a minute and finally found the tiny gift box that contained the necklace she'd purchased for Zina. She gently lifted the lid and peered at it for a long moment.

She wanted to ask Zina again to come with her, but she knew that wasn't fair. She would just give Zina the necklace, kiss her on the cheek, and tell her to keep in touch. Then, Stella would go home and try to get back to life as usual.

The thought of it made her sad.

Once she was ready to go, she knocked on Dana and

Lenny's door and let them know she was going to walk over to the lobby early to say goodbye to Zina.

Dana had nodded, her lovely face showing her concern. "You want backup?"

"No, I'm going to be ok," Stella said with a weak smile. Her throat was already getting tight.

Dana nodded and pulled Stella into a hug.

"We'll be in the lobby soon, ok?"

"Yeah, see you in a few." Stella took a deep breath, trying to banish the tightness in her chest, and started off toward the lobby.

There was an area off to the left of the check-in desk that hosted a massive tropical garden for guests to explore. Nowhere near as big as the one in the atrium, but still sizable. It had little winding paths and ponds with exotic fish and about a hundred lush, green plants that Stella had never seen before. Some weren't green at all, but had various shades of neon foliage that seemed almost designed to match the aesthetic of the resort.

She waited by the entrance to the garden's main path, her anxiety spiking by the second. She had left her bags at the front desk, except for her tote bag.

She was so fixated on watching the area by the desk that connected to the path to the atrium that she didn't notice Zina stepping up to her right side.

"Stella," her voice had Stella's head whipping toward her.

"Oh shit! Zina, you startled me!" Stella laughed, smiling up at Zina. She felt all sorts of emotions, but seeing Zina still made her happiness overpower anything else.

"I..." Stella began, but realized that saying 'I missed you' after being apart for a single day.

"I missed you," Zina said, pulling Stella into a hug.

It was somehow even weirder hugging a naked person when Stella still had her clothes on, but she closed her eyes and tried to memorize every little bit of how it felt.

When Zina finally pulled away, there were tears in Stella's eyes that she fought to keep in check.

"I got you something," she said, pulling the tiny box out of her tote bag.

"Stella, you didn't have to do that!" Zina said, looking genuinely surprised.

"I wanted to. It reminded me of you, and I wanted you to have something to show you how much you mean to me." Stella handed Zina the tiny box and watched as she gently opened it.

When Zina saw the dainty jewel inside, Stella noticed tears gathering in her eyes, too.

"The color made me think of your beautiful eyes," Stella said.

"Stella, it's perfect. Thank you," Zina said, smiling.

"I wanted you to have a gift from me that you can see and touch and remember that I'm sure about you. I'm leaving because that's what you've asked me to do, but it won't change the fact that I want to be with you. I want to see where this could take us. I know it seems fast, but lesbians back on Earth are known for this kind of thing," Stella finished with a laugh.

"Oh, really?" Zina asked slyly.

"Yeah, they call it U-Hauling," Stella chuckled.

"U-Hauling? That's ... not what I expected you to say," Zina laughed.

"It's not a long story, but I'll explain someday...when you're back on Earth with me," Stella said that last part while holding Zina's gaze. She wanted Zina to understand how serious she was about them being together again someday.

"Will you help me put it on?" Zina asked, holding the little box up. Stella nodded and took the necklace from its tiny cushion. Zina turned around and bent down slightly, allowing Stella to drape the necklace around her and fasten it. Stella placed a kiss on Zina's shoulder before she stepped away.

"There," Stella said, and Zina turned back around. The necklace looked lovely on her. Zina felt the tiny gem with her fingertips and smiled.

"Thank you, Stella."

"Want to take a walk in the garden for a few minutes? My friends will be here soon to board the shuttle home," Stella's throat was unbearably tight as she spoke.

Zina just nodded and took Stella's hand in hers.

They made their way through the little winding paths until they found a bench by a tiny fish pond. Zina sat first, pulling Stella down into her lap. Stella wrapped her arms around Zina's neck, leaning into her. She kissed

Zina's head, and they just held each other close for a long moment.

"You'll send me messages, right?" Stella asked.

"Of course I will," Zina said simply.

"How long..." Stella began, but trailed off because she didn't know what words to use.

"Let's just check in every few weeks about how we are both feeling about things. I don't want to make you feel like I don't trust you to know yourself and what you want, I just ... really want to be sure I'm not going to take over your life and ruin everything."

"I understand, Zina. If we do this, I want you to feel as good about it as I do." Stella put her hand on Zina's cheek and tipped her face up gently as she spoke.

"I am sure, though. And it's as true today as it will be a year from now," Stella whispered. She leaned down and claimed Zina's lips. Zina kissed her back, and Stella could feel all the longing in it.

"I should go," Stella said when they slowly pulled apart.

Zina studied her face as if she were trying to memorize it. Stella gave her a wistful smile and stood up.

They walked hand in hand back through the garden and out to the front desk, where Stella picked up her bags. Stella saw her friends gathered over by the gate for boarding the shuttle, so she pulled Zina into one last hug.

"Bye for now," she said quietly.

"Bye for now, sweet girl," Zina whispered.

A few of Stella's tears finally broke free, and she

wiped at them as she made her way over to join her friends. She wanted to look back at Zina, but she knew if she did, she wouldn't be able to leave at all.

THE SHUTTLE RIDE back to Earth had been just as surreal as the trip up to the space station. Stella still couldn't quite believe she had been to space. The fact that she had a smart, fun, beautiful alien mate was much easier to believe somehow.

When she finally got back to her apartment, she dropped her bags and plopped down on her large purple couch with a sigh. It felt nice to be back in her own space, but now all she could think about was all the ways Zina would fit here with her.

She looked over to her little kitchen and imagined Zina there, apron on, bending to slide a tray of cookies into the oven. When she looked out her window, she saw herself and Zina sitting in her bistro chairs, sipping coffee together and listening to the birds. She wanted all of it.

The next few days passed slowly. She and Zina exchanged messages at regular intervals throughout the day, and she fell back into her routine. She had her coffee in the morning and read her books, worked, and in the evenings spent time with Dana or one of her other friends. She went to pub trivia, sorted her laundry, and made a meal plan. She did all of the regular things–and through all of it, she wondered and wished.

She and Zina talked of everything and nothing in their messages. Updates about their days, random thoughts, noticing funny cultural differences–she liked Zina more and more every day. Stella found herself wondering if that feeling–right behind her sternum, warm and bright–was something more than liking.

And so, she moved through her life, thinking of Zina with every breath, imagining a future that she was starting to think she'd do just about anything to bring to life.

chapter sixteen

Zina rinsed the sticky fruit juice from her hands as she stared off into space. The water felt nice on her hands, and she was exhausted. She hadn't been sleeping particularly well since Stella had left three weeks ago.

"Zina," Reki said, too loud for how close they were standing.

"What? Sorry," Zina snapped out of her daze.

"You're a mess without your little human mate," Reki said, and handed her a towel.

"Yeah, well, apparently I'm biologically supposed to be mostly ok," Zina answered. She'd talked to Pazin about what to expect now that Stella was so far away. They'd said it might be uncomfortable, but it should get easier after the first week.

"Biologically, sure. Emotionally?" Reki gave her an incredulous look.

Zina scrubbed her hand across her face. "I think I made a horrible mistake, Reki."

"I mean, yeah. You should be with her, Zina! You deserve to be with her and give it a shot if that's what you both really want."

Zina knew her friend was right, but now Stella was back home, and she wasn't sure what to do.

Her device buzzed slightly to alert her of a message, and she smiled when she saw it was Stella.

How's the morning shift?

Zina loved talking with Stella about anything and everything. Over the weeks they'd been apart, she felt she'd gotten to know Stella, and she loved every new thing she'd learned.

So far, so good. I just stayed up too late watching videos about Earth again.

Oh really? What was this one about?

Puffins

Puffins?! Really?

Yeah, they're super cute. You don't happen to live near them, do you?

No, but I'll take you to see them. They go to a few different places.

Zina smiled at the screen, then looked up to scan the beach area to make sure the guests all looked content.

The little screen behind the counter, which pinged with communications from the resort or staff announcements, lit up and let out its delicate chime. Reki was closer, so they moved toward it, quickly scanning the screen to read the memo.

They looked over at Zina with a wry smile.

"What? Why are you looking at me like that?"

"The front desk is asking you to come down."

Zina immediately felt a twinge of panic. Was that where people got called when they got fired? Stars, she knew she'd not been on her A game, but she didn't think it was *that* bad.

"I'll be back as soon as I can," she said, standing up from where she'd been leaning against the counter.

Reki was still looking at her like they knew something she didn't.

"Take your time," they said, moving to continue putting away glasses.

Zina shook her head at her friend–she loved them, but they could be so weird sometimes.

She spent the entire walk to the front desk feeling halfway nauseated and anxious. She could go home if she really had to, but it would be a major setback. What would Stella think of her if she got fired?

Her mind was racing by the time she stepped into the lobby. She stopped short.

Stella was sitting on a bench not twenty paces in front of her. She smiled sheepishly and gave Zina a little wave.

Zina's throat was immediately tight with emotion that she didn't even try to contain.

She rushed to Stella and scooped her up in her arms, kissing her cheeks and all over her face, ending with a deep kiss on her perfect mouth.

"You're here," Zina said through her tears.

Stella laughed and nodded. "Yeah, I couldn't be away from you for another day, so I came back to get you."

Zina hugged her closer.

"I'm so happy to see you. I'm so sorry I was so stupid," Zina started, but Stella pressed a finger so, so gently to her lips.

"Shhh, it's alright. You don't need to apologize. You thought it was right, but I'm still sure Zina. I don't want to keep living my life like it was, just wishing you were there with me and waiting until we can be together. I want to be with you now. Do you want that too?" Tears were rolling down Stella's cheeks as she spoke. Zina let her words sink in, and suddenly, all her fears felt less over-whelming.

"Yes, I want that, Stella. I want to be with you always," Zina said and kissed her mate again.

"Good. Can I help you pack?" Stella asked, and the reality of what Stella meant fully sank in. Zina smiled wider than she ever had in her life, and gently set Stella on her feet.

"Absolutely, you can," Zina said. Stella beamed back at her.

"And then you'll come back to Earth with me?" Stella asked, taking Zina's hand in hers.

"Then I'll come back to Earth with you, sweet girl."

Zina decided she was really, really into Valentine's Day.

It was an Earth holiday that, she'd read, was named after some saint in a religion that no one really practiced anymore. It had been commercialized a long time ago, and the point of the holiday was to celebrate love in all its forms. Earth women had taken to celebrating their friends on the day before Valentine's Day, and then the day of was often focused on romantic love.

Zina couldn't get enough of all the red and pink and hearts and tacky, over-the-top glittery stuff. She loved it.

This was the first Valentine's Day she would have with Stella, and she was determined to make it special. She'd done her research.

It was cold where Stella lived on Earth, but Zina liked that, too. She snuggled her nose down into her fuzzy turtleneck sweater and pushed her hands further into the fleece-lined pockets of her coat. It wasn't a very long walk from the train station up to the quaint little house she now shared with Stella.

It was nice to be close enough to a big city that they could take the train in, but live far enough out that it felt like a small town. Zina was learning how to drive, but it was nice to still be able to get around in the meantime. She couldn't believe she'd been on Earth for almost a year.

Every day with Stella had been easy; even the days when one of them was having a hard time or they had some sort of conflict to talk through. With Stella, the rightness of it, and the truly good intentions they shared toward each other were at the foundation of their relationship. It was beautiful, and joyful, and comfortable, and Zina cherished it. She cherished Stella.

She arrived at her destination and pushed open the door of the tiny flower shop in their town. It was nice and warm and smelled heavenly.

The owner of the shop gave her a warm greeting–she was a frequent customer. Bringing her perfect mate flowers was one of her favorite things to do, so she was here every week or so.

This time was special, though. The shopkeeper handed her a massive bouquet of red roses interspersed with lush greenery and dainty baby's breath. She knew it was over the top, but she didn't care. She wanted Valentine's Day to be perfect for Stella.

The florist was her last stop–she had everything else she needed already at the house. It was going to be wonderful. Stella had been at her office for the day, so Zina had gotten everything ready to cook a steak dinner. She'd gotten the nicest cuts of meat, champagne, chocolate-covered strawberries ... the whole deal.

She also had a few other surprises up her sleeve—ones she hoped would make this first Valentine's Day together even more special for them both.

ZINA WAS lighting candles on the table when she heard Stella opening the door.

"Hi, sweet girl, welcome home!" Zina called, smiling.

"Hiiii," Stella answered in a singsong voice.

She came into the room a moment later, cheeks rosy from the cold. Zina savored the look of surprise on her face as she took in the scene. The table was set, the steaks were ready—everything was perfect.

"Zina! Baby, you shouldn't have!" She said, closing the distance between them and pulling Zina into a kiss. She savored the feeling of Stella's lips against hers, her scent filling Zina's lungs. Being close to Stella made all the tension leave Zina's body; she was home.

"It's Valentine's Day, of course I should!" Zina answered, squeezing Stella's hip. "Now let me take your coat."

She did just that, hanging it in their coat closet as Stella took her seat at the table.

"It smells amazing!" Stella said, beaming.

"Good! I hope it tastes alright, too."

"Stop it, you know you're an amazing cook," Stella said, still smiling.

Zina took her seat across from Stella and raised her glass.

"Here's to a lovely evening ahead to celebrate our love for each other," Zina said. Stella nodded, clinking her glass gently against Zina's.

Zina asked about Stella's day at the office, and Stella caught her up on all the drama while they ate. They laughed and talked about everything and nothing, and Zina tried to memorize the way the candlelight illuminated the soft, perfect planes of Stella's face.

When they finished, Stella tried to help clear the table, but Zina wouldn't have it.

"Stay there, or I won't let you touch me later," Zina said, eyebrows raised. Stella's mouth popped open, and Zina tried to suppress a laugh as she took Stella's plate.

Zina tidied up and grabbed the roses. She'd tied her card for Stella to a ribbon around the center of the bouquet.

"These are for you, my beautiful Valentine," Zina said, presenting Stella with the flowers.

Stella burst into joyful laughter when she saw how massive the bouquet was. "Zina! This is crazy!" She took them, obviously delighted with the ridiculousness of it.

Zina watched anxiously as Stella noticed the note attached. She reached into her pocket, ensuring that the tiny box was still there.

Stella untied the bow and pulled the card free, opening it. Her eyes scanned the words Zina had written (with great effort—writing in human English was harder than Zina had anticipated), and she could see tears gathering in her eyes.

Zina gently pulled the box from her pocket and got on one knee in front of Stella. When Stella had finished reading, she looked up to find Zina holding up the ring. Stella gasped, her lip wobbling, and her tears spilled free down her cheek.

"Stella, my perfect mate," Zina began, emotion clogging her own throat.

"You are the light of my life, brighter than every star in the galaxy. You are the center of my world, and I will always find my way to you. Being your mate and your partner has been the greatest joy and honor of my life, and I want to be yours in every way. I know that marriage is an important Earth tradition, and I'd like to call you my wife as well as my mate, and I want to be your wife, too. Stella, you are bright, and kind, and funny, and talented, and I love every single part of you. Will you marry me?"

Zina held her breath as Stella closed her eyes, but then she started nodding and dropped to her knees in front of Zina, throwing her arms around Zina's neck.

"Yes," came her muffled sob. "Yes, yes, I want to be your wife, Zina."

Zina hugged her back, tightly, and pressed a kiss to the top of her head. When Stella finally pulled back, her curls were matted to her wet face. Zina pushed the damp ringlets back and kissed her on the mouth.

After a long moment, Stella sat back on her heels and lifted the ring box from Zina's hand.

"Shit, it's beautiful!" she exclaimed. Zina smiled–she'd tried hard to get something Stella would love. In the end, she'd gone with a dainty, simple white gold band with a bright green sapphire cut into a teardrop shape.

"It's like the color of your eyes," Zina said, placing the ring on Stella's finger.

"It's perfect. Thank you, Zina," Stella whispered, leaning in to rest her head under Zina's chin.

"I love you," Zina said simply.

"I love you so much," Stella whispered.

They stayed like that for a long moment, just enjoying the moment, letting it settle into their memories.

"Zina?" Stella finally broke the silence.

"Yes, sweet girl?"

"Can we um...go upstairs maybe?" Stella looked up at Zina through her lashes, and Zina knew exactly what Stella wanted. She wanted it, too.

Zina didn't say a word; she just scooped Stella into her arms and headed toward the stairs. Stella squealed in surprise and then laughed, kicking her feet a bit as Zina walked.

Zina went straight to their bedroom and set Stella gently on the bed, bending to kiss her neck and jaw.

Stella hummed out a breath in pleasure, her hips shifting, obviously wanting some sort of friction. Zina would give her everything she needed.

"You're so pretty when you're desperate and writhing for me," Zina whispered into Stella's ear, letting her breath tickle. "I want you out of those clothes."

Zina didn't hesitate. She started stripping Stella down, piece by piece, revealing every inch of perfect creamy skin.

She kissed every place she saw, until Stella was moaning softly with each touch. When Zina finally had her undressed, she paused to admire the sight of Stella's glorious body.

"Stars, you're perfect, you know that? Every curve and dimple, I want to memorize it," Zina said, gently tracing a finger down Stella's sternum and across the curve of her belly.

"Zina?" Stella asked, her voice heavy with lust.

"Yes, my love?" Zina held her gaze as Stella ran her eyes over her still-clothed body.

"Two things," she began. "First, take your clothes off? Please?"

Zina smiled and slowly began stripping, first of her sweater, then sliding her pants down.

When she stood bare before her mate, she asked, "And the second?"

Stella smiled, and Zina saw the mischief in it. "My Valentine's Day gift for you." Stella rolled over and began to crawl across the bed toward Zina. It sent a wave of arousal through her, and she sucked in a breath, watching Stella move.

When Stella was right in front of Zina, she raised up to her knees so her face was nearly level with Zina's. She bit her lip and studied Zina's face again. Stars, this woman would be the death of her.

"Back at Galaxy View, you said you could get me pregnant with your tentacles because I'm your mate."

Zina nodded–this was old news. Stella had been on contraceptives since they found out.

"I stopped taking my contraceptive the other day," Stella whispered, running her finger across Zina's collarbone.

Zina's heart stopped. "What are you saying?"

"I'm saying that you didn't get me pregnant then, so you'll have to try harder."

Stella flicked her eyes up to Zina with a look more heated than any she'd seen on Stella's face before. Her words settled into Zina's mind.

"Oh fuck," Zina whispered, and claimed Stella's mouth.

They were a tangle of tongues, bodies pressed close as Zina pushed Stella back on the bed.

Zina reached her hand between their bodies, finding

Stella slick for her. "Shit," she hissed, every nerve ending in her body was alight, begging her to bury her tentacles in her mate. She felt her slit throbbing with her pulse.

She let her fingers find Stella's clit, rubbing gentle circles that she knew would get Stella's orgasm building. She bent down and sucked one of Stella's pink nipples into her mouth, flicking it with her tongue.

Stella moaned in pleasure, and Zina kept going, working her mate until a wet spot had begun to form on the bed beneath her. She wanted Stella to come.

Slipping two fingers inside, Zina increased her pressure on Stella's clit slightly and rubbed faster. Stella's breath caught, and she froze before her back arched, and she moaned her release.

"Good, pretty girl, you did so well for me," Zina whispered, savoring the feeling of Stella's warm cunt clamping down on her fingers.

When the final throes of her orgasm had passed, Zina rolled to the side of the bed and pulled out a plushy mat they kept under the bed. They'd found over the past year that some of the things they wanted to do were easier with the solid ground under them, but Zina refused to let Stella lie on the ground.

Stella was still panting, but she smiled when she saw that Zina had pulled their mat out.

Zina gestured for Stella to come over, and she obeyed, her cheeks flushed a beautiful rosy red. Her engagement ring glinted in the dim lighting, and it made Zina's heart swell.

"Lie down, pretty girl. I'm going to fill you, just like you asked," Zina said, and Stella lay down, her curls spilling out on the mat around her head.

"Spread your legs for me," Zina said, and Stella did, holding her gaze. Stars, she was so wet and perfect.

The sight was so erotic that Zina couldn't keep a hold on her tentacles any longer. They pushed out of her slit, and she groaned. Stella's mouth was open a bit as she watched, her pupils blown wide.

Zina took Stella's legs in her hands and pulled her hips gently up toward her. She could see Stella's chest rising and falling quickly, her breathing fast from the anticipation.

The tips of Zina's tentacles sought Stella's entrance, and Zina closed her eyes in pleasure at the first brush of them against her wet cunt.

Zina pressed her hips closer to Stella's and her tentacles pushed in, further and further, until all Zina could feel was the heat and tightness of Stella's walls around her.

Stella moaned, gasping at the fullness she must be feeling.

Zina moved, then, shifting Stella's legs so that she grasped both of her ankles gently in one hand. She shifted her right leg over Stella's hip for leverage and began shallow thrusts, working her tentacles deeper and deeper into Stella.

Zina thought she might die of pleasure. Her mate felt so good. She wanted Stella to come on her tentacles.

With her free hand, Zina began rubbing Stella's clit again, and her cunt immediately spasmed in response. Zina couldn't contain her orgasm, then. It came crashing over her in a wave, and she cried out. Her tentacles began to vibrate, and Stella swore and began to come too, following Zina right into an abyss of pleasure.

"Do you think I tried hard enough that time, or should we do it again?" Zina asked with a smirk.

Stella looked up at her, sweaty, smiling, and sated. "Hmm...I'm not sure. I guess better safe than sorry, huh?"

Zina laughed, and Stella did too.

She released Stella's legs and gently set them down, kneeling to bend over and kiss her. It was a lingering kiss, and Zina felt in that moment happier than she ever had in her life so far.

"I'm going to get you some water," Stella said when they finally came up for air. She sat up, kissing Zina's cheek.

Before she walked out of the room, she turned around and paused. "After that, though, we are definitely going to do that again."

about the author

Emma Elizabeth is a 30-something project manager living in North Carolina with her tiny dog. Writing queer romantasy, sometimes of the monster variety, is her passion.

When she's not writing or project managing, she enjoys playing video games, watching Lord of the Rings extended editions on repeat, reading, spending time with her girlfriend, and finding new hobbies to hyperfixate on. You can find Emma online here:

also by
emma elizabeth

Les Enfers Duology, Book 1 | In the Age of Blood

A queen who cannot die. A princess that wields death itself. Can they set aside their differences long enough to take a stand, or will they let their world slip into darkness?

When Aspen arrives in Les Enfers as the necromancer's emissary to the vampires, she steps into a world of intrigue and debauchery. She has one goal: secure an alliance with the immortal vampire queen of legend. It's the only way to save her people from the madness that's been slowly taking them.

Severine has lived for a thousand years, and never has she seen anyone as fascinating as the princess of the necromancers that waltzes into her life, demanding her help. Severine *wants* the little princess, but Aspen's hatred for her is obvious. If Severine

can't let go of the secrets she harbors, she risks starting a war--
and losing any chance she might have with Aspen.

A sapphic slow-burn romantasy set in a sweeping gothic world,
In the Age of Blood is the first half of the Les Enfers Duology.

Find this project now on Kickstarter!

Creatures of Domhan na Rùin series:

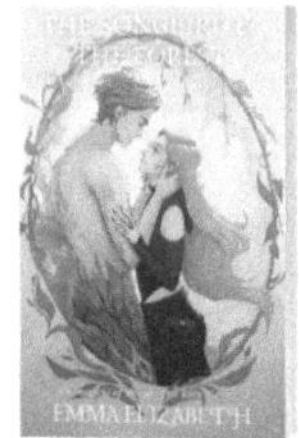

The Songbird & The Forest

Ilex the Dryad has lived alone in the forest for years, content
with only the trees for companions. Their greatest joy in life is
feeling the sun on their face, until a woman with red hair rides
into their forest astride a horse made of bone.

Dahlia is a necromancer who has a knack for crafting potions.
She's never really fit in with her more somber companions in
the Dead City, so when she is chosen to attend a celebration on
the other side of the continent, she's eager to set off and see the
world. What she doesn't expect is to find a beautiful Dryad and
maybe...a chance at a love like she's never known.

The Lion & The Thief

Mav is the Captain of the Guard of Zhava City; a petty jewel thief should not be causing her this much trouble. A string of robberies of Sartya's nobility has put her career at risk. As a Manticore, Mav has had to work hard to fit in with her human peers in the guard, and she refuses to risk all she has worked for by letting this string of thefts continue. Her thief is tricky though, and impossible to pin down...until one day a clue appears at the scene of the crime.

Colette returned to Zhava City three years ago to take care of her grandmother. After struggling to find employment, she decides to put her skills to use to redistribute the wealth of Sartya's nobility. It turns out she's a rather excellent jewel thief, but the savvy Captain of the Guard is on her tail now. Colette finds that she rather enjoys the Captain's attention.

The Siren & The Sea

After her bakery went up in flames, Maura left her homeland, Beitar, behind for the shores of the Vaporiad Sea. Though the locals warned her of the vicious sirens that made that coastline uninhabitable, she doesn't take their warnings seriously... until an unfortunate slip sends her tumbling into the brutal, icy waves.

Siren prince Anatolius never quite fit into the role his fathers expected of him. Though he is meant to spend his days monitoring the northeastern coast, he finds himself watching the curious human he discovered inhabiting the old fisherman's cottage. Watching her is the highlight of his day, until one afternoon he sees her fall into the unforgiving sea. He rushes to her aid, determined to get her out before the other sirens find her and punish her for entering their territory, only to find her as... an otter.

To keep Maura from facing the wrath of the other sirens, Anatolius claims she is his bride-to-be. The two must work together to navigate the delicate situation in the siren court and get Maura back home alive.

The Shadow & The King

Lunette has never failed a contract. As one of the most sought-after vampire assassins in Ichorna, she knows what she's doing when she accepts a contract to take out the minotaur king of Delkos. It's not her job to ask questions, but when faced with her target, she wonders if she should be asking anyway. Basilious tries to be a good king to his people, but his advisors have been pressuring him to secure an heir for the kingdom. He always hoped to find real love and partnership, but the reality of an arranged marriage or single parenthood looms. As the day he must announce his decision approaches, the last thing he expects is to imprint on a would-be assassin.

The Dragon & The Moon

Dorinavasya has spent a beautiful, if lonely, life as the goddess of the dark side of the moon. She is ill prepared for the mortal life she is thrust into when her sister betrays her, sending her to the world far below. Will she learn to experience the joys a mortal life can offer her?

Neamhaí has loved the dark moon goddess for as long as he can remember. Drifting through the cosmos with his fellow cosmic dragons, lending their starlight to the vastness of space, he has been content to love her from afar. When she disappears,

however, he knows what he must do–find her and protect her
at any cost.

The Magician & The Night

Coming soon!

Losian Rùin series:

Mistress of Hours

Two unlikely lovers find themselves entangled in a web of
dangerous secrets as they try to save a nation from its dying
magic. This fantasy romance is perfect for fans of From Blood
and Ash and The Plated Prisoner series.

Evienne is living her dream as the highest-ranking blood mage
in Ichorna when the queens assign her to monitor two

unexpected visitors from their elusive northern neighbor of shifters, Beitar. She can't help her curiosity when one of the visitors—a striking academic with piercing green eyes—seems determined to seduce her. What starts as a dalliance pulls Evienne into a web of centuries-old secrets that could turn her world, and her understanding of her power, upside down.

Orion, a professor from Beitar, arrives in Ichorna to attend their turn-of-the-millenium celebration with a singular goal in mind— he must find answers about his people's dwindling magic. He needs an Ichornian ally, though, and the alluring blood mage Evienne may be the key to his success. All his plans are upended, though, when an ancient magic awakes in his soul.

Despite their different allegiances, Evienne and Orion decide to work together to uncover the truth of Beitar's failing magic. As the horrible threads of the past unravel in the present, Evienne must choose between loyalty and her own integrity. The lives of a whole nation hang in the balance.

Lady of Souls

"Her kindness had never been weakness."

Léhiona Vass nearly gave her life to free her people. She awoke to a changed world; a world where the love she thought she had was a lie. With her magic and her will now freed, she has to decide who she wants to be. No longer silenced, Léhiona returns home to Beitar with Evienne and Orion, only to be berated by the new king for abandoning her duty.

Sinéad Lutair has never fit into the role of a lady of Beitar. As a guard of Beitar, it has been her duty to serve and protect her people. When her father arrives in his shifted dragon form with news from Ichorna, all of Sinéad's thoughts turn to her long-lost childhood friend, who left to sit upon Ichorna's throne for the good of Beitar.

Dangerous secrets lie in wait as Léhiona and Sinéad rekindle their friendship. The shifter magic of the Tuanadair has returned, but with a brutal new king and a missing Contrapensa, time is running out to uncover the truth. Léhiona's time to decide her fate is soon upon her, and all of Domhan na Rùin will be forever changed by her choice.

Lady of Souls is the second book in the Losian Rùin series, a fantasy romance trilogy that follows the women of Domhan na Rùin as they untangle ancient secrets and find love.

Preorder book 3 in the Losian Rùin series here!

Princess of Secrets

Dead City Novelettes:

Lessons with a Lich

When seasoned battle necromancer Iris arrives at the Royal Academy in the Dead City, she expects a few years of intense study to earn her degree. She did not expect to find herself struggling with her attraction to one of her professors, a lich nearly twenty years her senior.

After months of heated glances, will a romantic winter solstice be enough to bring them together?

Taken by a Gorgon

Princess Calla has never fit in with her family's expectations. Necromancers were meant for combat, but all she wanted to do was dance with the spirits. When she has finally had it with her mother's lectures, she takes off into the forest surrounding the Dead City to make her own way in the world.

What she did not expect was an encounter with a monster that would turn her to stone.

Nathaira had lived a solitary life after being cast out from gorgon society. She was content with her home, her art trade-- until her magic lashed out at an innocent woman. An innocent and incredibly beautiful woman. Nathaira quickly tangles herself in a web of lies and deceit that she has no way of undoing without hurting herself and Calla in the process.